While he drove, he thought about Sierra Benson.

Blake had been startled by their chemistry. He had overreacted by offering so much money, but when had a woman ever set his pulse pounding by merely saying hello?

Her stay at his ranch should be interesting. Maybe their attraction was something that only happened at a first meeting and wouldn't happen again. But with the smoldering chemistry between them, he couldn't keep from dreaming of seduction.

Dream on, he thought.

She was wrapped up in saving the world. She looked at everything through rose-colored glasses and saw everyone as filled with a basic goodness—which was not reality. This was a lesson he had learned early in life. Eventually, Sierra would learn that not everyone could be saved and all her sweet talk would be a memory. *That* was human nature.

No, she was not his type in any way—except for that hot, intense, mutual attraction. A scalding attraction he intended to pursue in spite of their differences.

* * *

Expecting the Rancher's Child
is part of Mills & Boon Desire's
Callahan's Clan series: A wealthy Texas family
finds love under the Western skies!

EXPECTING
THE RANCHER'S
CHILD

BY
SARA ORWIG

MILLS
BOON

First Published in Great Britain 2016
By Mills & Boon, an imprint of HarperCollins*Publishers*
1 London Bridge Street, London, SE1 9GF

© 2016 Sara Orwig

ISBN: 978-0-263-06498-8

Our policy is to use papers that are natural, renewable and recyclable
products and made from wood grown in sustainable forests. The logging
and manufacturing processes conform to the legal environmental
regulations of the country of origin.

One

Eagerness gripped Sierra Benson as the time arrived for her appointment with Blake Callahan.

She had done interior design for him, but that had been nearly two years ago and she'd never actually met him. Since she'd finished that job, and received a personal note of thanks from him, she'd changed careers. She was now director of Brigmore Charities of Kansas City, Kansas.

She hoped he'd asked to meet with her to make a contribution.

She'd read enough about him to know he was thirty-four, six years older than she was, a Texas multimillionaire, a hotel mogul and a rancher with interests in commercial real estate. Excitement bubbled in her to think their nonprofit might be getting a sizable donation.

Breaking into her thoughts, her assistant, Nan Waverley, announced her visitor's arrival.

"Send him in, please," Sierra said, as she stood and gave a pat to her light brown hair, pinned at the back of her head. She smoothed her straight brown skirt and looked up as Nan opened her office door.

"Thank you, Nan," she said—or that's what she hoped she said, anyway. Coming face to face with Blake momentarily took her breath.

She had seen pictures of Blake Callahan and knew he was nice looking, single and had an active social life, but she wasn't prepared for the dynamic man who, without one word, seemed to charge the air with energy as he entered her office. Even more startling, she was caught and held by brown eyes so dark they looked black. With their gazes locked, a sizzling current rocked her.

An even bigger surprise shook her when she noticed a flicker in the depths of his eyes. His chest expanded with a deep breath—he appeared jolted by the same magnetic charge that captured her. With an effort, she gathered her wits and turned away, ending the eye contact. She crossed the room to shake hands with him.

"Mr. Callahan, I'm Sierra Benson, and it's nice to finally meet you," she said, trying to regain her poise.

The handshake was a mistake. The instant his warm fingers closed over hers, the same riveting current jumpstarted again, only stronger this time.

Snagged by another exchange with his mesmerizing gaze, she stood breathless, aware of the physical contact, even more conscious that he was as immobile as she. How long did they stand in silence, held by a handshake and eye contact?

She slipped her hand out of his.

"It's Blake and, I hope, Sierra," he said easily in a deep voice. His tone sounded casual, friendly, but his look was probing, as if trying to find something that would explain why they were caught in an invisible current.

"Fine," she answered, striving to get a firm note into her tone. "Please, have a seat. I missed meeting you at the grand opening of your hotel because of a family emergency. Decorating your hotel was an exciting project."

Blake sat across from her, with her ancient hardwood desk between them. In an impeccable navy suit and a shirt with French cuffs that revealed gold cufflinks, Blake could have been a model—except he conveyed the signs of a man accustomed to more physical activity. He moved with an ease that indicated a high degree of fitness.

She suspected he had not been in any office in his life that was as run-down as hers. In his elegant clothes, he looked out of place in the eighty-three-year-old building that had not been maintained well. Tattered, faded books lined her shelves. The wooden floor had long ago lost its luster. Gusts of March wind rattled the aging windowpanes behind her.

"You did the best job on that hotel of any interior designer we've ever hired," Blake said.

"Thank you," she answered, pleased to hear that kind of praise.

"I was surprised to discover you've left the business when you have a natural talent for design."

"Thanks again. Helping others is my first love, so when this opportunity arose, I took it. We do a lot of good for people, which I'll be happy to tell you about. I assume that's why you're here." She settled back in her chair.

When he shook his head, her spirits plummeted. "No? Your response is an immense disappointment," she admitted. "If you're not here to make a donation, why are you here, Mr. Callahan?"

"It's Blake," he reminded her with a smile that momentarily made her forget business. It was warm, disarming and added to his appeal. She tried to focus and pay attention to what he was saying.

"I'm building a new wing on my ranch house in Texas. You're the best at interior design, and I'd like to hire you."

"I'd hoped you were here to learn about our charities and to possibly help in some way. I appreciate the job offer, but I have to decline," she answered as her disappointment increased. "I'm sorry you wasted time and effort to come talk to me in person." She smiled at him. "I wish you'd give me some time and let me tell you about all we do here to help those who need a lift."

"We have a problem," he said, studying her with those riveting eyes that scrambled her thoughts. "If we try, perhaps we can do both—I'll help with your charities and you consider my ranch job," he answered pleasantly, but she knew he was telling her he would listen if she agreed to what he wanted.

"I appreciate your offer. It's flattering, but I'm not leaving this work. It means too much to me. This was the work my grandfather loved, and before he died I promised to continue it."

"If you'd take this job, which would only be short-term, I could make it worth your while," he said, as if he hadn't heard her last remarks.

She smiled. He obviously did not take refusal easily.

"My interests are here," she replied. "You can find talented interior designers who can do your new wing," she added, wondering when he would give up trying to persuade her to do what he wanted.

They sat in silence a moment before he took out a checkbook and wrote. She suspected he would try to offer her more than the usual amount to do the decorating job for him. That aura of confidence surrounding him indicated he was a man accustomed to getting what he wanted. The money would be tempting, but she could find money elsewhere.

Certain he would offer an exorbitant sum, she watched as he wrote a second check.

Now he leaned forward, stretching out a long arm to place the two checks on her desk. "One of these is for your work on the new wing at my ranch. You'll have to live there to get the job done, but it shouldn't take more than a few weeks. The other check is a donation to this agency, and if everything is satisfactory, I'll make the same donation annually for at least three years."

Stunned, she looked at two identical checks, each for half a million dollars. For a moment she was speechless, trying to digest his offer.

"Why would you offer me so much money? There are other excellent decorators."

"I don't know them or their work. You're the best choice for the job. Besides, now that we've met, I'd like to get to know you."

Yes, there was chemistry between them—she couldn't deny it. But his admission that he'd like to get to know her only increased her reluctance about the job. She hoped to avoid ever being in a situation like her last job—where her boss tried to bribe her into his bed.

Staring at the checks on her desk, she forgot the past. She couldn't ignore the money Blake would pour into her nonprofit, and she couldn't stop thinking about the good that could be accomplished by his incredibly generous donation. And the promise of more donations to come. Her head spun with possibilities, dreams they had for the charity to grow. The kind of money Blake offered would take years to accumulate.

"You would really do this?" she whispered, looking up at him. "Just to get my design services?"

"Yes. And if it works out well, you'll get more donations," he said with a coaxing smile. As she looked at the check again, he sat in silence.

There was no way she could turn down such a dazzling offer that would put so much money into Brigmore Charities. It was thrilling to think how many people they could reach. Without looking up, she considered the man sitting across from her. She had seen his picture in society pages, Texas magazines and occasionally on television. He had an active social life, and a lot of the pictures had shown him escorting beautiful women.

"You actually live and work in Dallas most of the time, don't you?" she asked.

"One week out of each month I'm in Dallas, unless something important interferes. The ranch is where I prefer to be."

Realizing she might have to deal with him on a daily basis, she considered the job. In spite of his remark about wanting to know her, she could ensure they had no contact with each other socially. She suspected he received few rejections from women, but his sexual interests would not involve her. In spite of his personal remark, he would want her to concentrate on the job he had hired her to do.

The money he offered danced in her thoughts, with possibilities of how to use it to do the most good. There was no way she could turn him down, which she was certain he knew.

She nodded. "You win. I accept your offer. This is a marvelous, breathtaking contribution."

"It may be breathtaking, but it isn't solely a contribution—it's also payment for your work," he corrected with a slight smile, causing creases to bracket his mouth and making her pulse flutter. She had to admit he was appealing. Briefly, it occurred to her again that the huge sum might carry expectations of seduction, but she immediately dismissed the worry. He had enough beautiful society women in his life who were willing to keep him happy.

"I'll want to hire at least two people to assist me, and I'll pay them out of the check you've given me."

"No. I'll take care of their salaries. Just give me the bill."

"How soon do you want me to start?" she asked, still shocked by the sudden change in her schedule and the huge windfall.

"As soon as you can manage. Next week would be great. I'm anxious to get this wing finished."

She pulled her calendar close, though she knew she could start Monday. He couldn't be any more anxious to finish than she was, because as soon as she was done she could focus her full attention on Brigmore Charities' projects—and now she would have the funds to accomplish some of the agency's goals.

Years ago, the agency, started by Clyde Brigmore, one of her grandfather's friends, had almost gone under until her grandfather got involved, and with the support of her dad's church and her grandfather's hard work, the agency went from running a very small homeless shelter to supporting a larger shelter as well as a children's shelter. In the past year they had opened an animal rescue branch. Now many churches in Kansas City helped support the agency, along with individual donations, and most of her work focused on acquiring funding. It was work she loved, and through it she felt close to her grandfather.

She realized Blake was talking and she needed to pay attention. She tried to focus on Blake Callahan.

"Would you like that?" he asked, and she felt her cheeks flush with embarrassment.

"I'm sorry. It's difficult to get my mind away from

the changes in my life and the fabulous contribution you just made. What did you say to me?"

His dark eyes twinkled with amusement. "I'm glad you're pleased with our deal. I'm very pleased with it. What I asked was about transportation. If you'd like, I have a private jet. I can have you flown to Dallas, where a limo will take you to the ranch, which is about an hour and a half away from the airport."

"Thank you. I'll accept that invitation. If I start Monday, I'd like to arrive Sunday and get settled."

"That works. I'll be at the ranch, and I'll show you around."

She nodded, unable to keep from looking again at the spectacular checks.

"Then we have a deal?" he asked.

She looked up into black, fathomless eyes that seemed to hide his feelings. "We have a deal," she replied, feeling a tingle.

For a fleeting moment she wondered what she had gotten herself into. What would it be like working with him daily, staying in his home, having him constantly close at hand? The questions made her pulse race…but then common sense said he would turn supervision of the job over to someone and go on with his life.

In a languid manner, he stood. "If you have any questions, feel free to call me. Here's my business card and another number that's private. If you'll let me know your preference for what time of day you'd like to leave Kansas City, I'll let you know about the flight arrangements."

"Thanks. I can tell you right now, I'll be ready to leave after twelve Sunday."

"How should I contact you?"

She took a card off her desk and held it out to him. "My cell number is there, and you can always get me that way." As their fingers brushed, she had another flash of physical awareness of him.

She shrugged away the feeling as ridiculous. She couldn't understand the tingly reaction she had to him—that had never happened with any other man, but it was meaningless at this point in her life. She wasn't dating because she was focused on her work. This was a business arrangement, and she intended to keep her relationship with Blake Callahan professional.

She walked him to the door where he turned. This time she avoided offering her hand. Even so, as she stood looking up at him, dark eyes searched hers for a few seconds as they stood in silence. "This should be good for both of us," he said in a husky voice that heated her.

"I hope so," she said faintly.

He opened the door and stepped out before turning again.

"I'll text the flight arrangements and have a limo take you to the plane. The chauffeur will pick you up wherever you want."

"Thank you. That's a huge convenience. Until then, thank you for the donation, and the job and for having so much faith in me."

"I've seen the results of your work," he answered. He turned to leave and paused at her assistant's scarred desk, which had one leg missing and was propped up with bricks. He told Nan that he was glad to have met her, and then, smiling at Sierra and her assistant, he left.

When he had disappeared from sight, she turned to her assistant. "I'm going to take some time off. He's hired me to do a decorating job at his ranch."

"Mercy! I'd take that job, too. That's the most handsome man to ever walk through this office. Don't tell Bert I said that."

"Don't worry, I won't," Sierra said with a smile, thinking about her assistant director, Bert Hollingsworth, who was six years older than she was, with sandy hair he never could get totally under control and gray eyes that held a perpetual worried look. She had been friends with him since the moment they were introduced. Unlike her response to Blake Callahan, Bert had never once evoked any physical reaction in her.

Reassuring herself once again that she would see little of Blake once she was on the job, she tried to shove him out of mind.

"Will you please call Bert and then both of you come to my office? We have some things to discuss."

Giving her a quizzical look, Nan nodded and picked up a phone, repeating Sierra's instructions to Bert.

Sierra left her door open as she hurried to her desk and sat, taking the checks in hand to stare at them again in amazement. All that money—her head spun at the thought. She had promised her grandfather she would continue his hard work and help people when they needed help.

She had been raised to believe in the good in people,

and every week she had proof of that goodness from one person or another. Blake Callahan couldn't understand why she'd left interior design, but her career in nonprofit work was about what really counted in life. She had great faith in the ability of the human spirit to overcome adversity.

Shortly, Nan and Bert entered her office, Bert with his usual smile. "How'd the meeting go?"

"That's the reason I wanted to talk to you. He's hired me to do the interior design for a wing he's built onto his ranch house. I'll have to take a leave of absence."

"I thought you gave up that career," Bert said, frowning slightly.

"I thought so, too, but he gave me two payments—one for my work, and one as a donation to this agency. Here are the identical checks—each one for half a million." She passed the checks to Bert, who shared them with Nan. Bert stared open-mouthed while Nan read the amounts again. Nan's eyes were wide as she looked at Sierra.

"All that money to our agency," she whispered.

"Saints above." Bert shook his head, his eyebrows raised in surprise. "I knew the man was wealthy, but this—I never dreamed we'd get this kind of donation."

"I'm surprised you didn't faint," Nan said. "You don't even have to share that with your old design firm."

"No, but I'll share my personal check with Brigmore Charities. I'm also going to share with Dad and his church. Just think what good we can do with all this money."

"*I* may faint," Bert said. "No wonder you took the job. How could he want you that badly?"

"He thought I did a good job on his hotel. I turned him down at first, but I don't think the man is accustomed to hearing no. And there's more. If I do a good job, he will make an annual contribution of this amount to Brigmore Charities for the next three years."

Bert shook his head as if in denial.

"Is he single?" Nan asked.

Sierra bit back a smile. "Very. When I worked for him before, I heard gossip that he doesn't have serious relationships."

"I think you ought to use a little of that money for a background check on him. He wants you too badly," Bert said.

Sierra smiled and shook her head. "I don't think a background check is necessary. Look him up on the internet and look up his business. He can afford this check without thinking about it. His father is a billionaire, and Blake Callahan is wealthy on his own. There are a lot of women in his life. He has no need of me, except as a decorator."

"Want me to come with you?" Bert asked, a frown creasing his brow. Sierra held back another smile.

"Thanks, Bert. I don't think that's necessary."

"If for any reason it becomes necessary, you call me and I'll be right there."

"I will," she said, appreciating his offer, though it seemed ridiculous. "I won't be alone. I'm hiring two people to help me. He'll pay their salaries, and they'll live on the ranch with me part of the time."

"That's good," Bert said.

"If you need a secretary, don't forget me," Nan said, smiling.

For the next half hour they talked about depositing the check and presenting the donation to the Brigmore Charities' board of directors.

Finally, Nan rose to go back to her desk. Bert came to his feet, he closed the door and returned.

"I want to talk to you."

She sat behind her desk and waited.

"I don't think you should take the job or accept the check."

"You have got to be kidding," she said, staring intently at him. "Why on earth not?"

"He's up to something. That's too much money."

She held back a laugh. "I'll repeat—Blake Callahan will never miss this money."

"Why didn't he go to the New York agency he hired when you first worked for him?"

"He should have, but he said I did the best job he'd ever seen. He's accustomed to getting what he wants. He's flying me there in his private jet. Stop worrying, and start thinking about the best use for this money."

Bert shook his head and stood. "All right, but at the first sign of trouble, promise you'll call me. Let me know where this ranch is."

"I'll be fine," she said, smiling at him, knowing Bert had perpetual worries even when everything was rosy.

"If you're okay...what a windfall for us. This is going to help a lot of people. Our buildings are old and need repair—the homeless shelter was the original charity and it needs a new roof, new plumbing—all sorts of things. We have a waiting list for the orphaned children and their building and grounds need work."

"Plus the four-footed friends. Don't forget our dog and cat shelter. This will buy a lot of chow, and we can run some great ads. Maybe we can get a bigger place because what we have is so tiny we can only take a few animals at a time."

"True. I'll get busy."

"Good," she said and watched him go, leaving her door open behind him.

She knew Bert's worries were unnecessary, but there was only one threat from Blake Callahan.

That sizzling attraction that flared the first second they looked into each other's eyes. Never again would she get involved with an employer—yet how well could she protect herself from Blake's sexy appeal?

Late Friday afternoon Blake flew home to Dallas, where he had a small plane waiting to fly southwest to the tiny airstrip at Downly, Texas. At Downly he climbed into his waiting car and headed west to his ranch.

While he drove along a county road devoid of traffic, he thought about Sierra Benson. He hadn't met her when she did the hotel job, so he had been startled when the air sparked with a chemistry that he suspected she felt as much as he did.

Some of the most beautiful women he'd dated had never caused that kind of reaction in him. When he had taken Sierra's hand, the impersonal contact had had the impact of a blow to his middle, a tug on his senses that made him want to get to know her. His reaction to her had blown his intentions to hire her all out of proportion.

He had wanted her to handle the decor of his new wing because she was the best at interior design and decoration he had ever met. Add the intense physical appeal to her business skills, and he wasn't about to let her disappear out of his life. He had overreacted by offering so much money, but when had a woman ever set his pulse pounding by merely saying hello? Or shaking hands with him?

Her stay at his ranch should be interesting. He knew he had acted impulsively, and in what was an uncustomary manner for him, but he didn't want her to say no and disappear out of his life before he got to know her. He wanted to hold her, to kiss her. The thought set his heart racing.

Maybe their attraction was something that happened at first meeting and wouldn't happen again. With the smoldering chemistry between them, he couldn't keep from dreaming of seduction.

Dream on, he thought. She was wrapped up in saving the world and would probably be earnest, wanting marriage if there was a relationship.

They were from two different worlds—her whole aim in life was helping others, a commendable ambition, but not practical. At some point reality would hit, and she would give it up. Right now, it seemed ridiculous for her to toss aside a career she had a tremendous talent for to do charity work. She could have had her own design firm! Instead, she looked at the world through rose-colored glasses and saw everyone as filled with a basic goodness—which was not practical.

This was a lesson he had learned early in life when his father abandoned him. There was nothing good about a man who would dump his wife and small child, cutting them permanently out of his life. He never gave time or attention, and they had been hurt repeatedly by his indifference. Eventually, Sierra would learn that not everyone could be saved.

He'd learned about the realities of human nature at an early age, watching his father be honored for his philanthropy only to turn around and lie to get what he wanted, cheat on his wife and abandon his children.

Sierra would soon be like the rest of the world— as out for herself as the next person, and all her sweet talk about saving souls would be a memory. *That* was human nature.

No, she was not his type in any way—except for that hot, intense, mutual attraction.

A scalding attraction he intended to pursue in spite of their differences, because it was obvious she felt it too. He intended to clear his calendar and spend some time at his ranch while she was there.

He had planned on being at the ranch this week, anyway, so it would work out well with her starting Monday.

Then he would find out if that mutual attraction was a first-meeting fluke—or something more.

* * *

Sunday afternoon Sierra watched from her window as the plane lifted from the tarmac and gained altitude, revealing Kansas City spread below. Her gaze traveled around the plush interior of the aircraft with its luxurious reclining leather seats, tables between them, a magazine cabinet, a television screen and a laptop. The plane circled the city and headed south.

As she flew, she checked again to see that she had the phone numbers for two people she had worked with who now had their own New York agency. They had accepted her offer to work on Blake's ranch house, and they would start Monday.

Eli Thompkins was a quiet presence and excellent at interior design. She had admired his work before she graduated and gotten into the business, and she would be happy to work with him.

Lucinda Wells had started as an interior designer at the same time as Sierra. She was talented, specializing in contemporary design. Eli and Lucinda would look for art, paintings and sculptures, as well as furnishings. Sierra had already given them a few suggestions.

She'd taken care of the donation details with Bert before she left. She tried to focus on all the wonderful improvements and opportunities Blake's money would provide, but nothing could distract her from the tingly anticipation of seeing him again. Would she have the same sizzling reaction to him?

She hoped not, because that would complicate her job. Blake was far too cynical; his dismissal of her current work was proof of that. It was as if he was unable to see the goodness in others. She couldn't understand his outlook on life, and he didn't seem to understand hers. She needed to keep him out of her thoughts.

What was even worse, she hadn't slept well because of dreams that included Blake—dreams she definitely didn't want.

Had he felt anything when they'd met? Or had she imagined his response?

She suspected that by tomorrow morning she would have her answers.

Right on schedule, they touched down at Love Field in Dallas. She thanked the pilot and departed, crossing to the waiting white limo for another luxurious ride.

When they finally turned onto the ranch road, they passed beneath a wrought-iron arch with the name BC Ranch.

As they approached Blake's house, she saw barns, outbuildings and a sprawling two-story stone ranch house that had to have cost a fortune. Slate roofs glistened in the sunlight, and she could spot the new wing because of construction equipment still in the yard. In front of the house sprinklers slowly revolved, watering the lawn and beds of early spring flowers bordering the porch.

As she remembered Blake's midnight eyes and black hair, butterflies danced in her stomach. She hoped when they greeted each other she felt nothing except eagerness to start this job and gratitude for his donation.

The limo drove around the house, pulled beneath a portico and stopped. Blake stepped out and approached them. In jeans, a navy Western-style shirt and black boots, he looked like the successful rancher he was.

The driver opened her door and she stepped out of the limo. When she looked up into Blake's brown eyes, she realized this job would not be as easy as she had hoped, because a sizzling current rocked her to her toes.

How was she going to work with this tall, handsome man without giving in to this attraction?

Two

On a windy March afternoon, Blake watched Sierra Benson step out of the limo. She wore deep blue slacks and a matching shirt, her hair tied back by a blue scarf.

Taking a deep breath, Blake walked over and extended his hand. He wanted to find out if he had the same sensual reaction he'd had when he first met her, or if that had been his imagination. The moment his hand enveloped hers, he had his answer.

He felt the same sparks, and he saw the same surprise flicker in her big, blue eyes.

He never dated anyone he worked with, and she was not the type of woman he would be friends with. Even as he thought of the reasons he should keep his relationship with Sierra impersonal and professional, he was caught in those blue eyes and didn't want to look away.

Far from it. When his gaze lowered to her full red lips, he inhaled, trying to ignore a flash of curiosity. What would it be like to kiss her?

With a mental shake, he tried to get a grip on his thoughts. For all he knew she was engaged, deeply in love with someone at home and totally off limits.

"Welcome to my ranch," he said with a smile. "Come inside, and I'll have someone bring in your things while I show you around."

"Thanks," she said, slipping her hand out of his and falling into step beside him. "You have a beautiful home. It looks very big already, even without adding a wing to make it larger."

"It's home—a haven for me. I wanted a larger bedroom suite, something in a contemporary style, and there are three more large suites in the new wing. I wanted an entertainment room, an exercise room and a casual living area—so I'll have all that in the new wing, too."

"It's a huge place for one man."

He smiled. "I have a staff to take care of it and relatives on Mom's side of the family. They're scattered across the country, and she likes to have them here during Christmas—they'll fill both wings. I have three half brothers who visit and one of them, Nate, is married with a baby girl. Cade and Gabe—heaven knows if and when they'll marry. I have friends who come to fish or hunt or for a party or just to visit. I don't intend to rattle around alone. Would your family fill the space?"

Her eyes widened. "We could fill a lot of the bedrooms. Growing up, we always had kids sleeping on air mattresses and sofas because of the company we brought home."

He saw her looking at the heavy crystal-and-brass chandelier hanging over the circular entryway filled with potted palms. There were also oil paintings on the walls. The entryway ceiling was two stories high, and on both sides of the hallway the rooms were open, with Corinthian columns instead of walls on the side facing the circular hallway.

"I have an office you can use on the second floor. It's next to your suite." He motioned toward a sweeping staircase with iron railings.

On the second floor he directed her down a wide hallway. They passed a bedroom and then stepped into a living area. "This suite will be yours. If you need anything, just let me know." He saw amusement curve her mouth slightly. Tempting lips that looked soft and enticing.

Mildly exasperated that she stirred unexpected feelings in him, he shifted his thoughts to the present. "What's amusing you?" he asked.

"How could I possibly want anything in all this luxury?" she asked. "You've seen my office."

"Yes, I have. I suspect you didn't do the decor for it."

She smiled, and a warm feeling filled him. Her smile was contagious, as inviting as sunshine. "No, there is no decor in my office. Very plain vanilla, and we have buckets for rainy days."

"You should have enough money from my check to fix the roof."

"Probably, unless things come up that are more urgent."

Surprised, he glanced at her, realizing again that he didn't have any acquaintances like her. Neither his friends nor his family would put a charity project over repairing a leaky roof. She was a marvelous interior decorator, but he couldn't fathom her views of the world, her preferences. Again, he wondered how long this career would last for her. She would discover the reality of human nature and return to her old career. She would change, he had no doubts, but until then, her rosy view fascinated and confused him.

Hot chemistry or not, she was definitely not his type, and he knew with absolute certainty he wasn't hers. He needed to stop thinking about her lips.

"You have an adjoining bedroom and bath, and if you'll come with me, next door is the office."

She laughed softly. "It's bigger and better equipped, and far nicer than mine at the nonprofit. I might not go home." He saw the twinkle in her eyes and smiled at her.

"Nice office or not, I suspect you'll be ready to go when the time comes. Some who have a city background don't like the ranch after a few days. Or sooner—it's too quiet and isolated for them. Wear boots or take care when you're outside—we have rattlesnakes."

He waved his hand. "You have four computers with extra-large monitors, a copy machine, scanner, fax, a laptop, an iPad, a drawing board. If you need anything else, let me know."

"I think that covers what I might need, and I brought my own iPad." She turned to face him. "Blake, I want to look at the rooms we're talking about so I have an idea what I'll be dealing with. I've hired two talented people. When I unpack I'll give you their cards and a brochure about their agencies. Right now, they'll work out of New York, but they'll fly out here as we get to the later stages. That will mean they will need to stay nearby—"

"They can stay right here. There is plenty of room in this house and there are two guest houses. If you need or want anything, just tell me, or if I'm not here, tell Wendell."

A man knocked lightly on the door. He wore a black shirt, jeans and Western boots as he entered with her carry-on and a small bag.

"Perfect timing, Wendell. Sierra, this is Wendell Strong, who keeps the house running. Wendell, meet Ms. Benson, our decorator for the new wing."

After they exchanged greetings, Wendell set down her things. As he did, Blake added, "Wendell does a lot of jobs—butler and valet, but basically he's my house manager. With the exception of the cook, he manages my house staff and the gardener. His wife, Etta, is my cook."

"I'm glad to meet you, and thank you, Wendell, for getting my bags," Sierra said, smiling at him as he nodded and left.

"Have dinner here with me tonight," Blake said. "Etta has cooked all afternoon, so I hope when the time comes, you're hungry. I thought you might want to settle in now and catch your breath after the flight and drive. If you'll come down about six, we can have

a drink and relax a bit before dinner. After dinner I'll
show you the new wing."

"Sounds good, Blake," she replied. "One other
thing—we have a big picnic at home Saturday, so I'm
flying back to Kansas City on Friday afternoon."

"Sure. I'll take care of the flight arrangements for
you." He walked to the door and managed not to turn
around and take one last look.

As Sierra unpacked her few belongings, she couldn't
keep from comparing the ranch house to her condo,
which was large enough to be comfortable for her, but
not too big, and she thought about the home where she
grew up with her five siblings.

Her family's two-story house had been large enough
for her big family, kid friendly and nothing fancy. Always a place any of them could bring their friends, their
house was usually filled with company. Many meals had
included twelve to fifteen around their table.

Now, because of her work with Brigmore, she inter-
acted daily with people who needed help, and helping
them seemed so much more important than jobs like this
one for Blake. They were good people who had had mis-
fortune—illness or just bad luck. He was cynical, yet
ironically, his money would be such a help. Most people would appreciate the help, and use it to make their
lives better, something Blake didn't seem to believe.

She needed to get this job done and get back to Kansas City. She was attracted to Blake to a degree she had
never been attracted to another man before. He hadn't

done one thing to cause the attraction other than be himself, but she knew he felt it as much as she did.

His handsome looks and sexy appeal took her breath. While he seemed laid-back and easygoing, his air of supreme confidence was so strong it was almost tangible. He was sure of himself, accustomed to getting what he wanted, and it showed in his attitude, his demeanor and his walk. His assurance was obvious when he entered a room.

To her relief, he had been impersonal, businesslike, since her arrival. She hoped that didn't change. She appreciated him not flirting or trying to charm her. She hoped she could stay businesslike, too.

Yes, she'd agreed to dinner tonight, but after this getting-to-know you session, she hoped to spend as little time around him as possible. When she thought of the enormous check he had given her to get her to take this job, a staggering amount, she had to wonder what was behind that offer. Why had he wanted her that badly? She might have once been good at interior decorating, but so were others.

Feeling suspicious about his motives, she hoped he had paid that much for purely business reasons. She couldn't keep from thinking about the CEO she'd worked for previously. She had been an executive ready to move up when he had propositioned her, promising to make her a vice president if she would become his mistress. She hadn't seen that coming from him and he had held no sexual appeal.

His startling offer had shaken her judgment in men and angered her. Unlike with her CEO, a physical attraction had existed between her and Blake from the first second they had met.

She would have dinner with him tonight, get the layout of the new wing and find out what he wanted and then, hopefully, he would go on about his business. He didn't look the type to hover.

She showered and changed, dressing in a skirt, a matching red silk shirt and high-heeled pumps. She tied her hair behind her head with another silk scarf and went downstairs to meet him at six.

As she walked down the curving stairs, she saw him stop at the foot to wait. And watch her.

His dark gaze made her tingle. Taking him in at a glance, she smiled at him. He had changed, too. He wore jeans, boots and a different short-sleeve shirt that emphasized his dark, handsome looks.

"You don't look as if you've traveled most of the day. You look as fresh as the proverbial daisy," he said.

"Traveling in your private jet and a limo was not difficult or tiring. Both were about as comfortable as one can get," she said, falling into step beside him .

"Want to look around a little, or wait until later?" he asked.

"Now's fine so I'll have some idea where things are located and what kind of house you have."

"Let's go to the formal living area. It's rarely used, but I felt I needed it, and I know my mother would have been unhappy if we didn't have it."

"Does she entertain here?"

"Never on her own, but she's been hostess for me a few times. More in the past, when I first moved out here. This is it," he said, and she walked through double doors into a room with a marble floor, elegant furniture and chairs upholstered in deep blue antique satin and brocade. Ornate, gilt mirrors and original oils of landscapes hung on the walls. The vaulted ceiling was two stories high, and floor-to-ceiling glass comprised a wall of windows overlooking the front drive.

"This is beautiful, Blake."

"Thanks. The formal dining room adjoins this room," he said, motioning toward more wide double doors that were open. They entered a room with a large ornate crystal chandelier centered over a gleaming fruitwood dining table that could easily seat two dozen people.

Silver candelabra sat on a buffet with a sterling tea set. The stone fireplace and hearth were flanked by paintings of hunting scenes.

"This is another beautiful room."

"This one has been used more than that front room. I seem to have more dinner parties, although most of them are casual, the patio and backyard type. Much easier for everyone, and the food is still Etta's cooking."

"I think the cooking is what everyone remembers," she said.

They moved through a study, a library filled with books that he had not read, and she laughed with him over his plans to read them someday. He showed her a downstairs bedroom that had more ancient, beautiful furniture—old-fashioned, heavy pieces, hand carved and made of mahogany, including a four-poster bed.

"This is absolutely gorgeous, Blake."

"I think it's time for a drink, and later we can continue the tour. I have three more bedrooms on this floor, an office on the ground floor and another smaller one adjoining my bedroom upstairs. Let's go to the sitting room across the back. There's a bar and it's more comfortable."

She walked beside him into a room filled with light thanks to more floor-to-ceiling glass. It overlooked a patio, a garden and a kidney-shaped swimming pool of crystal blue water with a waterfall.

When he crossed to the bar, she scooted onto a stool across the counter from him.

"This is quite a contrast to your Dallas life," she said, gazing outside and seeing unending fields beyond his fenced yard.

"I love this place, and I need the ranch life. You've switched from New York City to Kansas City—still cities, but that's a switch."

"It's quieter, and I love my work now far more than what I was doing."

"I don't see how you can. You could have opened your own design firm, but now all your energy goes to people who won't thank you for it. You'll see. These people you help will just want more help again—no one really changes. This," he said, motioning to the expanse of his ranch home, "is where you can do something that will really last and be appreciated. You seem to have deep beliefs about how good people are—I'm sorry to say, you'll be disillusioned eventually."

"Blake, you're a cynical man. Look for the goodness in people. Believe in it, and you'll find it."

He smiled at her indulgently.

"You're looking at me as if you're going to pat me on the head and try to set me straight on what people are really like."

"That's a thought." He laughed.

She watched his hands as he poured drinks. He had fine, strong hands, which were probably good for ranch work. Maybe the isolation of this spread was what he preferred because he had a warped view of the world and a poor opinion of people in general.

When he held out a glass of pale white wine, she reached to take it, her fingers touching his lightly. He looked up, his gaze meeting hers. "Thanks," she said, taking her drink and sliding off the bar stool to cross the room and look at his pool. But she didn't see the water as questions swirled in her thoughts. Why did she have this intense reaction to him? Worse, why did he feel the chemistry, too?

"Running away from me?" he asked in a deeper tone as he joined her.

Startled, she met his probing gaze and wondered how long this reaction to him would continue. She didn't want to try to guess what he was thinking at the moment. It was impossible to miss the blatant look of desire in the depths of his brown eyes.

"We better stick to talking about business," she replied, wishing she didn't sound so breathless. How could she have this reaction to him when he wasn't doing anything to cause it, and when they held such opposing views of the world?

"Blake, we're not going there," she whispered.

Suddenly, he looked mildly amused, which shattered

the intensity of the moment. "Not going where, Sierra?"
Exasperation pricked her.

"You know where. I don't know why we have this
chemistry between us, but we need to ignore it, avoid
it and hope it will go away because I'm sure you don't
want to feel it any more than I do."

"I'm hurt," he teased, his eyes twinkling. "I didn't
know I was such an ogre that you don't want to find
me attractive."

"Right now, you're moving into an area where neither of us should go," she snapped, losing her usual
good nature and patience. She was on edge because of
her reaction to him, and his sudden flirting was only
adding fuel to the fire.

He laughed softly. "Relax, Sierra. I know our relationship is a professional one, but while you're living
here, we might as well indulge in some unbusinesslike
moments."

With an effort, she smiled and tried to bank her im-
patience with him. He had made light of that intense
moment, and she was certain it had meant nothing to
him. She wanted him to feel that it meant nothing to
her, too. She had no intention of letting him know the
extent of the edgy, sharp physical awareness she had
of him as a sexy, attractive male.

She suspected a man like Blake did not need any
coaxing to entice him into a physical relationship. She
was certain he had attracted females from a young age
and was fully aware of the effect he had on women.

"If that big check you gave me included anything

besides the design work you described in my office, then the deal's off."

Instantly the amusement left his expression. "Hey, Sierra. Absolutely not. My teasing was in fun and meant nothing."

She realized her reaction had been too strong. Her past biased her. She tried to relax, getting them back on a casual, friendly footing. "I don't know you well at all. Just making sure we understand each other," she said, smiling at him.

"Good. Have a seat. Etta is in the kitchen, and Wendell is helping her get dinner on the table. I'll introduce you to her. She's a fantastic cook, which always makes it easy to come home."

"You think of the ranch as home," she said a few moments later, after they'd stepped outside and were sitting in chairs facing his patio.

"I told you that I love it here. This is my haven. I can come out here and enjoy the total silence. Sometimes you hear the wind, and sometimes you don't even hear that. For a few minutes I can imagine the whole world is at peace. Even if it's not, my little corner of it is." He grinned. "Obviously, I like the ranch and I'm happiest here."

"You're fortunate. Far luckier than you give much thought to. I work with people daily who don't have a haven, not even a tiny one. Then, there are those who surprise me—one would think they couldn't possibly feel at peace because they own nothing, but they have an inner sense of a haven. That's resilience, and it's amazing."

"You really like working with those people, don't you?" he asked, looking more intently at her. He sounded surprised.

"More than anything. It's the most wonderful feeling in the world to help someone, or rescue an animal and find it a loving home, or make someone's life easier. That's the best possible reward."

"That's commendable, but in my experience people don't change. You can work your fingers to the bone and not make a difference. With the career you had, there were some very tangible financial rewards and lasting legacies. You could have built your own business instead of working with people who will disappoint and deceive you."

"You have a cynical view of the world. Expect more from people, Blake. There's a deep-rooted goodness in most people. Look for that and believe in it."

"I'm just puzzled. You've tossed over a spectacular, successful career, a fabulous reputation and a hefty income for something that will take infinite patience, probably have low financial returns and be a lot of hard work that sometimes goes unappreciated and unrewarded."

"Wow, Blake. That's strong. You're only looking at the downside of what I do."

"Just looking at it honestly because I can't understand your great faith in the goodness of human nature."

"I don't know what you've experienced, but I have seen that people are good and can live up to high expectations, or occasionally exceed them. Look at you.

You don't need money, yet you work hard to build your hotel business."

He looked away and was silent a moment. She noticed a muscle flex in his jaw and wondered why her question caused him to tense up.

"I want to know that I can be a success in the business world as well as in the ranching world. We all have our goals."

Wendell appeared, wearing a white apron over his jeans. "Dinner is served."

"Thank you." Blake stood. "Leave your wine. There will be some poured at the table."

She walked with him toward the front of the house, and then they turned into the wide hall. In minutes Wendell directed them to a kitchen that was big enough to hold her Kansas City apartment, but the tempting smell of beef assailed her before she ever stepped inside. Doors stood open to reveal stainless steel appliances and state-of-the-art cookware that, when not in use, would be out of sight behind the elegant dark wood. A tall, slender woman with her brown hair clipped at the back of her head, smiled. Etta wore a white apron over a black uniform.

"Sierra, this is Etta Strong, my cook. Etta, this is Ms. Benson, who is here to plan the decor for our new wing."

"So what's for dinner tonight?" he asked as soon as the women had greeted each other.

"Tossed salad with chunks of lobster, slices of avocado on the side and French dressing. Prime rib, asparagus hollandaise, mashed potatoes and gravy and buttermilk biscuits. With homemade peach ice cream," Etta answered.

"That sounds like a fabulous banquet," Sierra remarked.

"When you're seated, I'll get you started."

As Sierra walked with Blake to the adjoining informal dining area, she had another view of gardens and his irrigated yard, and marveled at the luxury of his lifestyle. She was thankful again for his check, and after their earlier conversation, she knew he needed to see some of the good his money would do.

They sat at a table that could easily seat ten. Wendell came with a bottle of red wine and one of white. He asked Sierra her choice and tipped red into her glass before pouring Blake's.

Etta set the prime rib in front of Blake for him to carve. She returned with a bowl of steaming asparagus that she served.

After the first bite of prime rib, Sierra sipped her wine and smiled at Blake. "I have to agree—you have a fabulous cook. This is delicious."

"Wait until you try her homemade ice cream. Wendell helps her with that."

"No wonder you like the ranch so much."

He smiled. "The food is the best, but there's more than food. Have you ever been to a rodeo?"

"No, I haven't."

"Actually, one of the best is in New York City, the Professional Bull Riders at Madison Square Garden," he explained.

"Do you ever participate locally?"

"Sometimes—not as much now as I used to. I have ridden bulls a couple of times, but not seriously. That's a bit rougher than I'm up for."

"Aw, shucks," she said, smiling. "So I won't see someone I actually know in a rodeo. The pictures I've seen look wild."

"That's the thrill of it," he said, and she laughed.

Through dinner, he was charming, keeping the same professional manner as if they were at a business dinner in Kansas City. Even so, there was an undercurrent of sensual awareness, and every minute spent in his company drew her closer to him and heightened his appeal.

As Wendell removed her dinner plate, she smiled. "My compliments to the chef. That was one of the most delicious dinners I've ever eaten. I don't know which was best—that prime rib or those fantastic biscuits."

"Thank you," Wendell said, smiling as he started toward the kitchen. "I'll tell Etta."

Sierra looked at Blake. "I meant every word of that. What a marvelous cook you have."

"I do everything I can to hang on to both of them. Etta has a reputation throughout the county—and probably farther than that. If she decided to leave, she would have so many offers, I don't know how she would decide."

The peach ice cream was served with white chocolate chip cookies, and they lingered over coffee, which Sierra barely touched. Once again, she thought about the homeless people at the shelter and how they often lived with hunger. Blake's check would provide food for so many, and again, she felt enormous gratitude for his donation.

"Etta should open a restaurant—talk about natural talent for a job."

"Don't put ideas in her head," he teased.

"Did she cook for your family before cooking for you?" she asked. For a fleeting second, she saw a hard look cross his features. It was gone so quickly, she thought she must have imagined it.

"No. The family she cooked for decided to move to South Texas and sell their ranch. I was friends with her son growing up. We're the same age and went through school together. He's a great guy. After graduation from high school, he went to the Air Force Academy and now flies fighter jets. He's stationed in Europe. They have four other kids who are scattered except for an older, married daughter who has four kids. She lives in Dallas, and the grandkids come out here a lot and stay with Etta and Wendell. They're cute kids, and we have horses for them—except the little one, who's too young to turn loose yet."

"That's great. Were you born and raised in Dallas?" she asked. This time she had no doubt about the shuttered look she received.

"Yes. My father divorced my mother before I was a year old. He severed all ties with us, so I grew up without knowing him. He has never been a part of my life. If he's ever spoken to me, it was before I was old enough to remember. I don't know why, but my mother has never remarried."

He spoke in a flat voice, and she realized she had

touched on a sensitive area. "I'm sorry, Blake," she said, meaning it, unable to imagine how devastating it would be if her father had rejected her. She thought about her generous, loving dad who had always been a big part of all his children's lives.

Blake's voice dropped, and she heard a note of amusement. "Sierra, don't ever play poker. You look like you'll start crying over me any minute. Of course, if you want to hold me close and try to console me for being abandoned—"

"Forget it, Blake," she interrupted, laughing at him. "I see you survived and grew up quite well."

"I'm friends with my father's other sons, my half brothers, now because the oldest one and I went to school together. He's a little younger, but we played football together in high school. Enough said on that subject. Where are you from? New York?"

Still thinking about his abandonment by his father before the age of one, she shook her head. "No. I'm from Kansas. That's why I came back to work in Kansas City. My dad's a minister, and I have a big family with a lot of contacts in the city. My mother is a retired teacher, and most of my family is involved in charity projects related to my job. Mom and two of my sisters volunteer at our animal rescue shelter. Dad runs some programs to help people from the shelter get to church. He has free breakfasts at his church every morning... I could keep going. There are six kids in my family, fourteen grandkids and a foster grandchild—soon to be adopted. I'm the one with no kids."

"That's a big family. It's a very different lifestyle

from my background, where I grew up with just two of us at home—Mom and me."

"We were always free to bring our friends home with us, so we constantly had a house filled with kids," she said, unable to imagine a home of just two.

"Don't look at me like I was left by myself on the street," he said with a grin. "I'm not one of your charity projects, although that might be interesting."

She smiled in return. "There is no way I could see you as a charity project at any point in time. I suspect your mother showered you with love, and you had friends galore."

"I always thought so," he answered easily. "Let's move and let Etta and Wendell clean up and go home."

"Sure. I want to step into the kitchen and tell Etta how wonderful dinner was. I can't imagine having someone like that cook for you all the time."

"It is another draw the ranch holds, although if I had to live in Dallas year round, I'd try to get her to move with me. Wendell, too, of course."

Blake waited while she went to the kitchen to tell Etta and Wendell again how wonderful dinner had been. She returned to find him leaning one shoulder against a door jamb and looking at her legs. His gaze flew up to meet hers, and there was no mistaking the blatant sexual speculation in his expression.

Trying to ignore the unguarded moment, she crossed the room to join him, and they walked into the big living area overlooking the patio and pool.

"Tell me when you're ready, and I'll show you the new wing. We can take a quick look tonight and go over the rooms in detail tomorrow—or we can skip anything related to work tonight and let you relax."

"I can relax while I work. If you care to, you can show me around tonight. I don't mind at all."

"Come on and we'll look," he said and they headed for the stairs. "Tomorrow I'll give you blueprints and pictures, so you'll know what I want. The workmen aren't completely finished with construction, but they're far enough along that they'll finish this week. By the time you're ready for the actual work, they'll be gone.

"I told you about the additions earlier. Also, I had an elevator put in because my grandmother visits, and she is getting less enthusiastic about stairs. Mom has her own one-story house on the property, but she rarely spends time there. She's in Patagonia, sightseeing with friends now, or I would have had her join us for dinner. Here we are—we'll walk through, and then if you have questions, fire away."

As they strolled down a wide hall, she was more aware of the tall man beside her than of her surroundings. Their footsteps in the empty, unfinished wing created a hollow sound. When they entered the first suite, she saw that the rooms would be light because of the abundant windows.

She could smell sawdust and new lumber. She was equally aware of the faint scent of Blake's aftershave, the scrape of his boot heels on the new hardwood floors, of his nearness when he opened doors for her and stepped back to hold them.

Thankful she wouldn't be working with him on a daily basis, she couldn't shake the acute awareness of him. As they stood in the large living area of the suite, he turned to her. "Downstairs in the older part of the house I showed you some of the rooms. They all have formal French-style furniture, European antiques, plus one suite holds two-hundred-year-old furniture I bought at an estate sale in New Orleans."

"The rosewood furniture that's ornate and elegant. It's beautiful, Blake," she said.

"Thanks. I think so. I did that mostly for my mom because she loves that kind of furniture, and she was influential in the selection of the earlier furnishings. Up here, I'd like a change in decor. I'd like these suites to be contemporary with sleek lines, open spaces. That's more my style."

"That's popular now, and there are some beautiful furniture designs available," she said, walking through the empty rooms while he followed. "You'll have plenty to choose from."

"Whoa," he said. "Sierra, I'm turning this project over to you. I want you to make the decisions about the decor—that's your field, and I trust you totally. From here on, you take charge. Do your stuff, get it lined up and then show me. I do not want to be too involved."

"Suppose you don't like it?" she asked. "People usually want to see some of the early planning. You had people who checked on what I was doing at your hotel."

"That's because you'd never worked for us before. Now the early stages will be your deal. I've told you contemporary, and we'll set an upper limit for the cost.

I don't want to be consulted until you've made some selections and have sketches showing how it'll look."

"That's flattering, and you're the boss," she said. "At least you know what you want."

"Damn straight," he said quietly, his voice acquiring that husky note that indicated furniture was no longer on his mind. "I know exactly what I want," he said.

"All right, Blake. I'll see if I can please you," she flung back at him. Her pulse raced as she turned to walk away. When she did, her back tingled, and she felt his gaze on her. Telling herself that it was probably her imagination, she had no intention of turning to see if he was studying her.

The suites in the new wing were roomy, each unique, one with arched, wide windows giving a panoramic view of his lighted pool.

As she turned, she once again caught Blake gazing at her with a lustful look. She met his gaze and the moment intensified, her surroundings disappearing, leaving only the tall, handsome man facing her.

Her heart pounded as she left the room. "I'll move on," she said over her shoulder without glancing back.

They had only started looking and had the rest of the wing to finish. She drew a deep breath, determined to keep her mind on business. Not so easy when she was beside him or when she caught him looking at her with unmistakable desire.

Again, she was grateful that he didn't live on the ranch full-time.

They looked at suites with large rooms, lots of glass and open spaces, big walk-in closets and bathrooms large enough to hold several pieces of furniture besides the usual bathroom equipment. She could envision some beautiful suites.

"You'll have a hotel when you finish," she said, amused. "This would even be big for my family."

He smiled. "I like plenty of room. I do have company, and I have family now, thanks to Cade and my other half brothers. When they come to visit they need their own space. I told you before, Nate is married. He's two years younger than Cade. He has a beautiful wife and a beautiful little baby daughter who is about two months old. They are back east right now, visiting her parents."

"Is Cade the one close to your age?"

"Yes. Cade is the Callahan I know best. He's the oldest of the three. Gabe is the youngest."

While they talked, she gazed into his dark brown eyes. She was aware of how close he stood, and she considered initiating conversations only when standing across the room from him. This intense reaction was unique, disturbing and something she couldn't understand. She turned to walk away, reminding herself to keep a professional distance between them.

"That's it," he said finally when they finished. "It's early. Let's go downstairs and talk for a while. You'll live and work in my house temporarily, so we might as well get to know each other."

She knew now was the moment to politely decline, but looking into his midnight eyes, she couldn't. "For a while," she said, unable to resist accepting his invitation. What was it about him that held so much forbidden appeal?

As they walked downstairs, he asked, "Want anything to eat or drink? We have desserts, more ice cream and an after-dinner liqueur. What would you like?"

"Just a glass of ice water, please," she said.

They went to the sitting room at the back of the house, and he stepped behind the bar to get ice water for her and a beer for himself.

As she sat in a straight wingback chair, he sank down on a large brown leather chair facing her, sipped his beer and set it on a table. "Do you plan to stay with the nonprofit, or will you go back to decorating someday?"

"I plan to stay where I am. A project I have dreamed about is finding foster parents for homeless kids—now with the funds you provided, maybe we'll be able to start that program. You would have room to take one," she teased.

He gave her a startled look and then smiled, the corner of his mouth lifting a fraction. "That's commendable, but a little kid right now wouldn't fit in with my lifestyle."

"Nonsense. You can hire nannies, maids and tutors, whomever you need."

"I think you're yanking my chain. If I take in a child, it won't be to turn them over to staff to raise."

"I'm glad to hear that," she said, not telling him he surprised her. He didn't look the type to be interested in child care. "My brother and sister-in-law have a two-year-old foster child right now. They've already started adoption proceedings, and the agency is helping them. She's a precious baby."

His black eyelashes were thick, slightly curly and

added to his handsome looks. Was it going to be difficult to work for him? Even if he weren't her boss, his cynicism didn't fit her worldview. Perhaps his dad's rejection had brought about Blake's sour opinion of people. She couldn't expect any of her arguments to change his mind. Because of that, she didn't want to get involved with him, no matter how intense his physical appeal.

"Is this your brother's first child?"

For an instant she stared at him blankly, and then remembered their conversation. "No, she isn't. They have three other girls and a boy."

"That's overwhelming."

"Not really. They wanted a family, and they have one they shower with love, but they feel they have room for another baby." She paused. "You said you're not planning on marriage anytime soon..."

"Not even remotely. I'm wound up in my career, and I'm not a family man at this point in my life." He paused as if lost in thought while he shook his head. "Right now I don't want a serious relationship. If I ever get romantically involved, I'll have to give it a lot of thought and time before I make even a small commitment. You don't sound as if you're into serious relationships, either."

"That's right. I suppose for the same reasons as you. I'm immersed in my job and want to build our agency. Since I'm single, I can devote a lot of time and energy to getting things going. Also, with the money from you, we can get our programs on more secure footing and increase our outreach. You should try my profession sometime," she said, half in jest.

He was too cynical about people to get involved in the details of helping others, but maybe she could make him see the good she was doing, the good his money would be doing. "You've already helped, but you could help more, maybe even on a small scale. You could easily start a program on your ranch for homeless kids, and you wouldn't have to involve yourself any more than you'd like to get involved."

He gave her another crooked smile. "Don't try to talk me into saving the world. That isn't my thing. I give in plenty of ways."

"How much do you give of yourself, Blake? Try just once, and maybe you'll see why I feel the way I do. Maybe you'd see the goodness in people."

"Money will be a bigger help than my presence."

"Blake, I've never known anyone so cynical."

"Call it cynical. I call it realistic."

Her gaze lowered to his mouth. What would it be like to kiss him? When she glanced up, his brown eyes were intent on her, as if he could guess her thoughts. She felt her cheeks grow warm. As she turned away, she heard a clock chime. "My word, it's one in the morning," she said, picking up her empty glass. "I need to say good-night."

Standing, he grinned. "You don't have to be anywhere at any specific time. You're in charge of the schedule. As for me, I'll be up and out of here before dawn, and then I'll come back to answer any questions you have about getting started."

"Thanks for your confidence in me. You're leaving lights on," she said as he walked beside her.

"I can turn them all off from my room when I turn on the alarms."

As they climbed the stairs, they talked about the new wing. He stopped with her in front of her door and turned to face her. He stood close, once again holding her full attention. She forgot the hour, the place, everything around her. She forgot the incredible differences between them. All she was aware of was the handsome man facing her with an expression that made her heart race.

He reached behind her head, moving languidly, his fingers working at the silk scarf knotted behind her neck. Each faint brush of his warm hand against her nape stirred tingles. He tugged lightly, and her hair fell free with long strands tumbling slightly below her shoulders.

Sinking in brown eyes, she couldn't get her breath and her heart drummed. *Step away...step away...*repeated steadily in her thoughts, a silent warning that she couldn't possibly heed. His mesmerizing eyes sent another message. He intended to kiss her.

Never before had she crossed that invisible line between business and pleasure, but she couldn't back away now or even dredge up a protest.

"I don't know why we have this volatile chemistry between us," he said in a husky voice, "but we do. It's impossible to ignore. Sooner or later, I'm going to kiss you. I figure it might as well be sooner and get this attraction settled," he said as he slipped an arm around her waist.

Why couldn't she walk away right now—set the right

precedent? Common sense whispered that now was the time. This was what she had intended to avoid, yet she couldn't pull away.

Her heart clamored for his kiss. Curiosity made it inevitable. With the hot attraction between them, what would it be like to kiss him?

She couldn't answer her own question. She had to take the risk to find out.

Three

Immobilized by his declaration, Sierra felt her heart thud. She placed one hand lightly against his forearm, feeling the hard muscles that indicated physical labor. He definitely did not spend most of his time in his Dallas office.

He stepped closer, and then leaned down as she finally managed to whisper, "We shouldn't—"

He brushed her lips with his, a faint, feathery touch that stirred a longing for more. Her insides heated while her heart pounded faster.

"We shouldn't," he whispered, "but we're going to." He kissed her before she could say anything else.

For a second she stiffened, and then she slipped her arm around his shoulders and placed her hand at the back of his neck while she kissed him in return. With his tongue stroking hers, he drew her tightly against him. He was solid, flat planes of rock-hard muscle against her softness.

She tumbled into heart-thudding passion. For a moment all caution vanished, replaced by yearning for more of him. She wanted to touch and kiss him, to forget all her warnings to herself. She longed to let go and make love. What chemistry did they have that set this sizzling desire burning between them?

His kiss stopped logic and caution, and made Blake the most desirable man she had ever met. It created a bond between them that she couldn't easily—if ever—forget.

How long did they kiss? She didn't know, but finally common sense resurfaced.

Gasping for breath, she stepped back. He was also breathing heavily, gazing at her as if he had never seen her before. A sinking feeling enveloped her. She had opened the proverbial Pandora's box.

"We have to forget that happened," she whispered.

"There's no way in hell I can forget that kiss," he replied.

"You'll have to. We're working together. The dinner was wonderful. Good night, Blake," she said, then stepped into her suite and closed the door.

Her heart pounded. How was she going to work with him? How could she keep from falling in love with him? She had left her last job not only to pursue her dreams but also to get away from a sexual situation with her employer. Now she had taken a job where she had a far bigger problem with her employer—she wanted him.

The fleeting thought of quitting was gone as fast as it had come. His donation was too big, the possibilities too great to turn him down.

She would just use caution and stay away from him. He was a busy man with many interests and friends, including women who should be far more appealing to him than Sierra was.

Taking a deep breath, she walked through her suite to get her cotton pajamas and get ready for bed. She couldn't imagine sleeping. Every inch of her body tingled. An intense longing to be in his arms was paramount and hopeless to try to shove out of her thoughts. Her lips still tasted of him, and it was as impossible to forget his kiss as it was to ignore the electrifying attraction between them.

Could he sleep? Or was he tied in knots with desire too?

She couldn't think about what Blake felt—that would only make the situation worse. She hoped he realized they both needed to back away. Blake was a charmer, but his deepest feelings and views on life were the opposite of hers. He was hard, cynical and didn't believe in the goodness of others. During dinner he had talked about his feelings on commitment and the career she'd left behind. He didn't understand her views at all.

For her own good, she had to stop this before it went any further.

She had hoped to avoid ever getting into a sticky situation with a boss again. Yet going against all logic and planning, she had kissed Blake—but she had no intention of letting that kiss escalate.

There had been attraction with her last boss, Alex Deagens, too, but it had been more about friendship. She'd liked Alex—until the night their relationship changed.

They had worked late at the office and were the only people there. Alex had kissed her. When he paused, holding her, he'd told her he would get her a fancier apartment and promote her to vice president if she slept with him.

Shocked and betrayed by his proposition, she'd refused and left in haste.

Feeling gullible and foolish, she'd spent a sleepless night. First thing at the office the next day, she turned in her resignation. Within the hour she was told by someone from Human Resources that her resignation had been accepted immediately and she did not have to stay the rest of the month as she had offered.

That experience with Alex shook her judgment about men, and afterward she had backed away from getting involved with anyone romantically. She didn't accept dates.

Even so, she still believed anyone could change. Her new career allowed her to focus on the good in people, and occasionally provided the chance to offer life-changing acts of kindness. That absorbing work, plus moving back to Kansas City to be close to her family, kept Sierra too busy to miss not having a social life outside of her family. But now she was here with Blake. This was a man for her to avoid. Already she knew any emotional entanglement with him would only end painfully. By placing monetary success above helping the less fortunate, he missed out on the best parts of life.

She thought about his father abandoning him when Blake had been a baby—a hurt that had to have left permanent scars. No little child could understand a father who walked away. That had to have been devastating, and perhaps was the reason Blake seemed to be tough and hard. Again, she was thankful for her loving father, a man who had always been a part of his children's lives.

She needed to get this job done and get home, away from Blake and the consuming attraction that resonated between them.

Business and pleasure didn't mix well. He was her boss, albeit a temporary one, and she needed to remember that. She had to stay professional, get the work done and go home where she could forget him.

And forget their kiss. Hopefully Blake already had.

Blake left for his gym and indoor pool. He swam laps, hoping the activity, the cold water and the lateness of the hour would combine to drive Sierra out of his thoughts and cool his body.

The hot chemistry they'd felt since the first moment seemed guaranteed to fulfill its promise of passionate, raw sex—at least as far as their kiss was concerned. He still burned with longing to make love to her. Kissing her had not eased his desire for her at all. Instead it set him on fire with need for more. If she was responsive with a kiss, what would she be like in bed?

The thought tied him in knots and promised a night of little sleep.

Of all the women he had known, she was the most unlikely to generate lusty longings. She was the daughter of a minister, a lifelong do-gooder whose goals were foreign to him. How could she give up a brilliant, successful career for one with so little return? Her income would be only a fraction of what it could have been. Why would she want to live that way and make such unnecessary and thankless sacrifices? He knew too well the bad blood that could arise between people, the lasting hurt that could be caused. The only thing he trusted was his bank account—something that gave solid returns, including power and a fortress against hurt from trusting the wrong people.

He didn't need or want a future with Sierra. All he wanted was to seduce her, to get her into his bed and make love for hours, to find out if that sizzling chemistry would take them all the way.

Thinking about her, about their kiss, aroused him. Never in his life had he experienced the same intensity of attraction, and it made no sense to him.

With a groan he swam faster, trying to get her out of his thoughts, to wear himself out and cool the hot longing that tormented him.

As much as he wanted to make love to Sierra, he knew the sensible thing would be to stay away from her. Let her do her job and go back to her charity work. That was the intelligent thing to do because she would want commitment. This was not the woman for him, not even for one wild night of making love. His body wasn't listening to his brain, though. In spite of knowing what he should do, he still wanted seduction.

He continued swimming until he was exhausted. After he showered and dressed in the gym, he ran five miles on the treadmill. Hoping he had done enough so he would drop into bed and be asleep in two minutes, he returned to his suite.

He passed her door and remembered both kissing her and her response with vivid clarity. He had a sinking feeling sleep was a long way off.

Blake slept a couple of hours and woke long before sunrise. He dressed, grabbed a bite of breakfast and left the house as if chased by goblins. He needed hard, physical labor, or at least to be outdoors and moving around, to work with others who would take his mind off Sierra.

As he walked his land by the light of the moon, he wondered whether she had slept. Would she be able to concentrate on work? He had to laugh at himself. His kiss might not have unnerved and aroused her to the same extent as it had him. She might have slept peacefully and right now be working away without a thought about him.

"Pompous jackass," he called himself quietly. "Forget her."

She was an employee, and he needed to keep a professional relationship with her. Actually, he needed to stay the hell away from her. He had already paid her a ridiculously exorbitant sum and committed himself to donating to her agency for the next three years—he should have left her office and pulled his wits together before he wrote those checks. He could imagine his accountant's questions. The only honest reason Blake had paid such princely sums was because he wanted to see more of her. There wasn't any other way to explain it. If he kept pursuing her, what other mistakes would he make?

Blake swore quietly. She had jumbled his thought processes—something he couldn't recall happening with any other woman. He couldn't understand himself and the reaction he had to Sierra. She was a gorgeous, appealing woman, but he was friends with more than a few who fit that description. And she was definitely not his type.

But if she was so much not his type, why couldn't he shake her out of his thoughts?

Later that morning, Blake drank coffee and ate a muffin, leaving the house and intending to find some kind of ranch work that was so demanding, he wouldn't think once about Sierra.

Shortly after 9:00 a.m., he returned, showered and went to find Sierra so they could go over the blueprints for his new wing.

When he knocked lightly at the open door of her suite, he saw her standing in the office. Smiling, she motioned him to enter.

"Come in."

"Good morning," he said.

With a lurch to his insides, his gaze swept over her, taking in her hair pinned high on her head. Her pale blue shirt and coordinating slacks heightened the blue of her eyes. He wanted to cross the room, wrap his arms around her and kiss her into a frenzy of desire.

Instead, he paused at the door of her office, glancing beyond her to see the monitors showing the floor plans of various rooms in his new wing.

"You're already at work," he said. "Did you have breakfast?"

"Oh, yes. Etta was in the kitchen and I had a delicious breakfast—eggs Benedict, melon and berries, and orange juice. I assume you were out working."

"Yep, I was. How's it coming here?" he asked.

"We're just getting started. Let's look at each suite and you tell me if there's anything I need to know," she said, walking to the computers and pulling a chair close so they could look at the same monitor.

He still intended to let her make the decisions, but he sat beside her because he wanted to be close to her, and this was the only way. He caught a faint whiff of her perfume, something light, barely discernible, yet enticing. Everything about her was enticing and he inhaled deeply, trying to focus on what she was saying to him. He looked at her long, slender neck, fighting the urge to run his fingers lightly over her skin and trail kisses under her ear.

With an effort he studied the computer screen and tried to squelch all lusty inclinations—a hopeless ambition when he sat only inches from her. The chemistry between them shook him.

With grim determination he stared at the monitor and tried to forget that she sat beside him. She seemed unaware of their attraction this morning, but he wondered what would happen if he brushed her hand with his or leaned closer when he asked her a question.

Unable to resist, he decided to find out. "Shift to the west bedroom," he said.

When she paused to find the one he was talking about, he placed his hand over hers and moved the mouse. "There," he said. He pointed to a balcony off one of the bedrooms. "This is on the west, and I've ordered an awning for it. Out here in summer that afternoon sun will be fierce."

He was barely thinking about what he told her. He had heard her quick intake of breath and knew she was responding to the physical contact, just as he had.

The knowledge was electric. He wanted to forget business and kiss her again, but he could not and would not.

For the next hour he maintained a professional manner, keeping his distance. She managed to be just as cool and detached, and if he hadn't heard her deep breath when his hand covered hers earlier, he would think that she barely noticed him as anything other than her client. They would not have a lot of time together before she would be working on her own and then going back to her Kansas City office. Once the job was over, he wouldn't see her at all.

He turned to her. "While you're here, you might as well see a little bit of Texas, some local life. Do you eat barbecue?"

Smiling, she nodded. "Yes, and I imagine Etta is as good at cooking barbecue as she is at cooking prime rib."

"She is, but this time it won't be Etta's cooking.

There's a rustic barbecue restaurant in a small town near here. I want to take you. How about this Thursday night, since you said you're leaving Friday?"

Something flickered in the depths of her eyes, and there was a few seconds' hesitation that made him think she would refuse, but then she nodded. "Barbecue Thursday night sounds great," she answered cautiously.

It had been a spur-of-the-moment invitation, but now his anticipation grew because she had to have debated with herself whether or not to turn him down—and she had said yes.

"Eli and Lucinda will arrive tomorrow afternoon and fly back to New York Wednesday."

"They can have suites here. I'll tell Wendell so everything will be ready for them."

It was midmorning, and he was already eager for the evening.

He knew he should leave her alone. But he couldn't help thinking that maybe, this time, there would be more than a kiss between them.

After a quail dinner that night, Sierra went to the kitchen to compliment Etta. When she turned to leave, Blake took her arm lightly, another one of those casual contacts that she shouldn't even notice, much less want. Now was the time to tell him good-night and get out of his presence, except she wanted to stay with him.

"Let's sit on the patio. It's a perfect night. There's no wind, and it's pleasant and quiet."

"Sure. That was a marvelous dinner. It's the first time I've eaten quail."

"Etta knows how to cook game birds."

"Blake, this is lovely," Sierra said, enjoying the cool spring evening, the pool with a splashing fountain and beds of red and yellow tulips in bloom in front of a backdrop of pink japonica and yellow forsythia. "Do you sit out here a lot?"

She saw a crooked smile as he shook his head. "Only with company. Otherwise, I always feel too busy. I expect to take the time, but I don't ever get around to it."

"That's dreadful. You're missing wonderful, peaceful evenings. What about when you and your brothers get together on holidays?"

A cold look filled his eyes, and he shifted his gaze away from her, looking over his yard. "We're getting together more and more, but still not always on holidays. Growing up, until I was in high school, I was never part of their family. Our mothers were never on friendly footing, and my mom and I were cut off from even knowing them all the years I was a little kid."

"I'm sorry," she said, meaning it.

He smiled. "I had a good childhood. You look as if I'm one of the big disasters you need to help."

"I know better than that, but I'm sorry about your family. Family is the biggest part of my life."

"Mom showered me with love and kids accept life as it comes."

"Oh, yes, they do. I just thought you and your half brothers were close from the way you spoke of them."

"We are now, thanks to Cade. If our father comes to Texas, I stay away. He and I don't speak—or, to put it more accurately, he doesn't acknowledge me," Blake said, and this time she heard the flat tone of his voice that she guessed hid anger and hurt.

She thought of her own big, close-knit family, and realized that while Blake was enormously wealthy, he didn't have some of the simpler things in life that were far more important to her.

"How did you ever get to be friends with Cade if you grew up without associating with him—or am I asking too many questions?"

"No, you're not," he answered, his voice remote and casual. "I think I mentioned we both played football in high school so we were thrown together a lot. We got to be friends, and he introduced me to his brothers. All of us played ball. Our parents were out of the picture a lot at that age, and we all became friends. When we got to know each other, none of them had any hostile feelings toward me, and I didn't have any toward them."

"That's great, Blake," she said, glad that he'd found those relationships even though his father hadn't acknowledged him. "I think your father made a huge mistake when he cut you out of his life."

"I certainly thought he did," Blake said lightly, smiling at her. "Enough about the dad I don't even know. So who's the guy in your life, Sierra? Do you have anything serious?"

"Nothing serious, and there's really no guy right now. Since I moved back and started working with the nonprofit, I'm so busy. I have a few friends who go out together on Saturday nights, but most of my time is spent with family. There's no one special. There sort of isn't time right now."

"I can understand that," he said, stretching out his long legs. "Ditto for my life. I have friends, but I'm busy and I travel for work. I figure someday that will all change, but right now, I'm deeply involved in my business. These are the years to build a career."

She smiled. "I think that last is a bit of advice directed at me in particular."

"I try not to lecture, but yes, it is. I'll never understand the choices you've made. You could have invested your time, energy and money in a business that would grow and hold value. Instead, you've invested in people—you'll never know if they've done the right thing with what you've given them. They may not even be grateful."

"I don't feel that way about my work. I guess you don't understand mine and I don't understand yours," she said lightly, but meaning every word. "So you have the biggest and best chain of luxury hotels. Will they keep you happy when you're not working? Will they entertain you? No family, no love, no companions, no laughter and fun. All you have are hotels and money. Makes no sense to me."

"I told you—this won't go on forever. I'm young, energetic and ambitious, and I want to build my chain of hotels now. There's time for love and laughter later when I have a fortune. I have moments when I enjoy myself and the others in my life. I know how to have a good time. Let's take last night for instance—"

"Never mind," she interrupted hastily and shook her head, smiling. "I remember last night without you bringing it up again. No matter how much we talk about our views, I doubt we'll ever understand each other."

"Maybe not," he stated, leaning closer and lowering his voice. "But that doesn't mean we can't have a great time together or become friends. There are times when I enjoy life to the fullest, and I suspect you do also."

Tingles raced through her as she saw the hot desire blazing in his brown eyes.

"I'm amazed you took tonight off from work and social appearances," she said, knowing he had a very active social life that was chronicled in papers and Texas magazines.

"I can forget completely about work when I want to," he said quietly, his voice dropping another note. He stood and closed the distance between them, grasping her wrist lightly to pull her to her feet.

Startled, she gazed up at him as his arm circled her waist and he leaned close to kiss away what she had been about to say.

Her heart thudded the instant his mouth covered hers. For a fleeting moment she started to push against him and step away, but then she was lost in sensation, spiraling away in a kiss that made her heart race.

Hot kisses made her want more as she ran her hands across his strong shoulders. When his palm drifted lightly over her breast, she gasped with pleasure and strained for his touch.

She didn't know how long they kissed. She was lost in him, his hands moving over her until she felt his fingers tugging at her blouse. Holding his wrist, she looked up at him. "Let's back up," she whispered, trying to catch her breath while she stepped out of his embrace. "This isn't why I'm here."

"You're the one who told me I'm missing out. That I need to learn how to really enjoy life. I can't think of a better way to enjoy it."

She walked away from him, straightening her clothes. Then, with space between them, she turned to face him. "Let's enjoy the conversation tonight. We can get to know each other."

"You're ending some of the sexiest kisses I've ever experienced. Or maybe you don't find them so sexy."

"I'm not answering that because you're pushing me into more kisses."

"It was just a statement—nothing more."

"Do we sit and talk, or do we say good-night and I go to my suite?" she asked.

"We sit and talk," he answered, taking a deep breath. "As a matter of fact, let's get a cold drink. What would you like?"

"I'll have iced tea," she said, and watched him move to a bar and fix her drink. She crossed to perch on a barstool as he worked. She felt as if they both needed a moment to get away from the past few minutes. "So tell me more about who you see staying in these rooms in this new wing?"

He smiled, and she knew he guessed her efforts to shift their attention back to business. "I see myself staying there. It could become easy to see you staying if you wanted. Would you like that?"

She laughed softly. "I will not be staying in your new wing and you know it. If you don't want to talk about that, tell me about your newest hotel."

"A twenty-story tower in Orlando," he said, opening a beer for himself and walking around to motion to her. "Let's go sit where it's comfortable. C'mon, we'll go inside now. It's chilly this evening."

When she sat in a tall, brown leather chair, he pulled another closer to her. They had a small table between them. He took a sip of his beer. She drank some tea, and then turned slightly toward him.

"The hotel in New York that I was hired to do was close to one of your father's hotels. I'm surprised to hear you don't see or talk to him, because your hotels are so close. I figured you worked together, or even each owned a share of the other one's chain. That must not be the case."

"No, it definitely isn't," he said so quietly that a chill went down her spine. A subtle change came over him, giving him a hard, cold look.

"Your father's hotel was older, so it was built first," she said.

"Yes, it was." As he gazed at her, she realized he had built near his father's hotel on purpose.

"Do you have any other hotels close to your father's?"

"Yes, as a matter of fact. And yes, I've built by his hotels on purpose."

Shocked, she stared at him. "That sounds as if you are competing. Is this a battle between the two of you? Does he ever build close to a hotel you already have?"

"No, he doesn't."

"So, it's only you building where you will give him competition," she said, looking at him intently. "He's so successful—aren't you making it more difficult for yourself? Competition goes both ways."

"I hope I've done a better job than he has, and frankly, I hope I've made a dent in his hotel business. My hotels are bigger, newer, have more amenities and are more luxurious, so I'm sure you've got the picture—I intend to put my father out of the hotel business," Blake said quietly. "I'm building an empire that I want to make larger than my father's. It is a competition I intend to win."

She stared at him. "You're doing this because of the past—because he left you when you were a baby," she said, unable to imagine that life mission. "You're out for revenge." He intended to get even with his father for old wrongs. The idea was so removed from her way of life, she could only stare at him as if she had never seen anyone like him.

"You're bent on revenge—the absolute opposite of all that I hope to accomplish," she whispered without realizing she had spoken aloud. "You'll ruin your life, Blake."

Four

"Nonsense," Blake answered easily. "My father has billions. I won't hurt him, because he has other endeavors and a fortune that I can't possibly diminish significantly. Nor do I want to."

"Then what's the purpose? Why would you spend millions, your time and your energy in pursuit of something destructive that can't possibly help you or him?" They viewed the world so differently. She realized again that she would never understand Blake.

"I want him to know that he has a son who exists, who is a good businessman and who can do a better job at some things than he can. Hotels are only one part of his fortune. My chain isn't a big deal to him, though they are good business for me."

"That makes it seem even more futile and a waste of your time."

"No. My hotels are making a tidy sum for me. My hotels will pay your salary."

"I'm glad there's something besides revenge as a motivation," she said, still shocked to discover his purpose.

Her gaze swept over his thick black hair, straight nose, penetrating eyes, firm jaw and wide mouth. Her heart skipped a beat as she recalled their kisses last night. He was so handsome, so appealing, yet so very wrong in seeking revenge.

She knew that no matter what was happening between them, after this job, she would tell him goodbye, go back to her routine and never see him again. They had no common ground, no part of their lives they could share. Sexy appeal and hot kisses were not the foundation of solid relationships.

Though her body might try to convince her differently, this was a man she did not want in her life. As she studied him, he leaned closer, moving his chair until their arms touched. Blake brushed her cheek lightly with his warm fingers. She shivered, momentarily forgetting their differences, responding to the feathery contact.

"See what I can do," he said softly. He placed his fingers lightly on her throat and raised his eyebrows. "This between us goes beyond our differences. When we touch, the world and our differences don't even matter."

"Yes, they do. Maybe for a short time we can forget

them, but they're real and stronger than thrills from kissing." She took a deep breath, trying to recall why she needed to pull back from him. "I thought you said you're close to your half brothers. You'll hurt them if you hurt your father."

Blake smiled at her. "No, I won't. They know what I'm doing and they know I will never do any real damage to my father. It's a point of pride. And, frankly, my hotels are making money for me. Our father has ignored all his sons to some degree. They all know what I'm doing, and they don't care. He's hurt them, maybe more than he's hurt me, because he gave them more hope that he would be in their lives."

"Is he close with their mother?"

"They're friendly. They speak. My mom and dad are definitely not friendly. He cut her out of his life abruptly when he cut me out. She hasn't spoken to him since I was three or four years old," he said, taking a pin out of Sierra's hair.

"He has remained in Cade's life, and in the lives of his other sons and sees them once or twice a year, but he was never much of a father. Financially, he provided for them, but they all went to boarding schools and got little of his attention or time."

"That's entirely different from my family or how I grew up," she said, catching his hand where it was wrapped in her hair. "You probably shouldn't do that," she whispered, aware of his fingers and the slight tugs on her scalp, of his dark gaze on her.

"Be thankful you didn't grow up the way we did," Blake said in a cynical tone. "All his sons—all of us—

are wealthy in our own right, and my half brothers will inherit more wealth from him. I'm not taking any of that away from them. What I'm doing is like a flea bite on a dog—annoying, yet meaningless to my father. It only means something to me."

"Perhaps, but you're aiming all your energy at revenge," she said, horrified by the current goal in his life, and how readily he admitted it. "We're total opposites," she said, thinking about what he was telling her while at the same time aware of his fingers moving in her hair, taking it down, letting her locks tumble over her shoulders.

"I suppose we are, and I guess that's why it's so difficult for me to understand why you gave up your interior design career. You have a master's degree. How can you toss that aside? That took you years, and a lot of work, to achieve. You could make a fortune, make a name for yourself—why throw that away?"

"Because what I'm doing now is more important to me. There are people in the world who just need a little help. There are animals that are abandoned and hurt. That's what's important to me."

"I think you'll have regrets."

She shook her head. "I don't think so. I'm just amazed at the choices you've made. Maybe someday you'll rethink what you're doing."

He leaned close. "Maybe I will, or perhaps you can convince me to do so," he said in a sexy, coaxing voice that made her think about hot kisses and forget all about careers and revenge. "Want to take a shot at reforming me?" he whispered, brushing his lips over her ear, fanning her desire.

"I can't convince you to do anything," she whispered.

"You'd be surprised how easily you can convince me to do some things," he whispered back, leaning a fraction closer while his gaze dropped to her mouth. She could barely get her breath.

"Blake, stick to business." Could he tell her heart was pounding? She should move away from him, but she was immobile, held by light kisses and feathery caresses. "Blake…"

His mouth covered hers, and his fingers combed into her hair, pulling her closer as he kissed her—a hot, passionate kiss that drove everything from her thoughts except desire. She wound her arms around his neck, forgot her resolutions to keep her distance, no longer cared if he sought revenge on the father who abandoned him. For the moment, heat poured into her and she wanted his arms holding her tightly against him.

Blake picked her up, placing her in his lap. He leaned over her, shifting to cradle her against his shoulder while he continued to kiss her senseless.

Her fingers played over him, running across his broad shoulders, down his thick biceps, across his broad chest. How could he turn her world topsy-turvy, making her forget reason and toss aside caution, causing her to risk her heart when he could so easily break it to pieces? She knew she should stop him. But it was long past the time to say no.

Instead, she held him tightly, kissing him wildly, pouring herself into kisses and caresses while she trembled with the need that he built as he caressed her in turn.

As he tugged at her buttons, she wriggled away and stood, gasping for breath. He came to his feet. His shirt was undone, open to reveal his sculpted chest.

"We should say good-night, Blake."

"I'll go with you to your room," he said.

"No. I have some reading to do, and I want to get my notes in order."

He leaned close to whisper in her ear. "You're scared to stay down here with me for another hour tonight. You won't work on your notes."

She laughed softly. "You might be right. You're a physically appealing man, Blake Callahan—something I didn't consider when I took this job."

"Physically appealing," he repeated. "That may keep me up all night, as well as the thought of more kisses."

"It's been an interesting day and evening, and the dinner was grand. Thanks."

"You're welcome. I'm enjoying having you here."

"I'm enjoying being here. You have a beautiful home."

"It's going to be even more in line with what I want when this wing is finished. I'm ready for a change."

"Have you thought about a change that might go deeper than rooms and furniture? Perhaps turning your energy and focus in another direction?"

"I do believe you are trying to reform me," he said, looking amused as he ran his fingers lightly over her shoulder and smiled.

She couldn't resist, and smiled back. "Doesn't hurt

to try. Have you ever thought about just calling your father and trying to make peace? You're a grown man now. He might be happy to meet you and talk to you. Have you spoken to him since you became an adult?"

Blake tugged a lock of her long hair gently and then curled it in his fingers. "You're trying to reconcile me and my dad. That won't happen at this point in my life. I've tried to talk to him only once. I was three or four, and he had to talk to my mother. A limo waited, and when he came out, I tried to get his attention. My mother stepped out, carried me back into the house and closed the door. He never said a word to me that I remember."

"Blake, that's dreadful. He missed out on so much that he can never get back."

"That isn't how he saw it, I'm sure. The court left my mother financially well off, so I had a good education, but my father was never any part of my life. What's worse, he was only a small part of his other sons' lives, even though he definitely played dad to them. I told you, I knew where I stood. They didn't. They kept hoping for more from him. By the time I was five, I knew better than to expect even a hello."

"That's sad," she said, thinking again about her father and how much a part of his children's lives he had always been, and now how good he was with his grandchildren. "Your father cut so much joy out of his life."

Blake smiled at her. "You live in a rosy world, Sierra."

"No, I don't. I see people every day who are hurting and have needs—health, income, relationships—their situation isn't rosy. Children adapt, so all of you accepted not seeing him as part of your lives, but he cut himself off from love from all of you."

"How did we get back on the subject of my dad? Damn. There are better things to talk about. And a lot better things to do," he said in a thicker voice as his gaze lowered to her mouth.

Her heart drummed. She wanted his kiss, even after spending the past hour learning that he was a man bent on revenge.

She shouldn't kiss him. She shouldn't even stay the rest of the week on his ranch. She could work from her office in Kansas City. She was set up here with all kinds of electronic equipment and could work all week undisturbed, but here she would see Blake. With the attraction that burned between them, she should be packing her bags now.

If only she could remember how opposite they were and not be dazzled by hot kisses, flirting and sexy smiles.

If only she didn't respond to his slightest touch, to just being near him. A week and then they'd part—surely for one week she could keep her heart and head intact.

As she looked up into midnight eyes, she knew she was making promises to herself she couldn't keep.

She lowered her gaze to his mouth and then looked back up to his brown eyes.

"Sierra," he said quietly, sliding his arms lightly around her waist and leaning down to kiss her.

Standing on tiptoe, she kissed him in return, shutting off all thoughts of packing and leaving. She just let go and enjoyed his kiss.

Soon enough they would say goodbye permanently, and a few kisses tonight wouldn't matter at all.

His arms tightened as he leaned over her and his kiss deepened, becoming more passionate. He ran one hand through her hair, down her back and then over her bottom, under the hem of her skirt and along her thigh.

His warm hand, barely stroking her, drifted up along her leg and then moved between her thighs. Gasping, she clung to him while she thrust her hips against him. He was aroused, hard and ready.

"Blake, slow down. We're going too fast for me."

"We have something here, and we both like it," he replied gruffly.

"Kisses aren't enough," she whispered, clearing her throat. "Goodnight, Blake." She stood on tiptoe to brush a kiss on his cheek.

"Sure you don't want to come to my suite, have another drink?"

She laughed. "I'm sure, but good try. Such a subtle approach," she added, shaking her head.

He grinned. "I keep waiting and hoping you'll ask me into your suite. I'm good company at night."

She laughed. "I'm sure you're fabulous company, and I know you have the best kisses this side of the Atlantic Ocean, but I have to say good-night." Smiling, she brushed his cheek with another kiss and went up to her room.

Picking up her phone, she saw two messages from Bert. He had worked late, which wasn't unusual. Far more than any of her family, Bert worried about her constantly, and she had answered half a dozen text messages since she'd landed on Sunday. Sending him another reassuring text, she placed her phone on a bedside table and hoped she didn't hear anything more from him until tomorrow.

Long after she went to bed, she lay in the dark, thinking about all Blake had told her about his dad. There was a tough, hard side to Blake. She could see why. She didn't think he had chosen the right way to deal with his father, but she could understand his anger.

She sighed because she was certain Blake would have no part in calling his father or doing any such grown-up thing. He was bent on revenge, and she couldn't sway him. She had no intention of sticking around to try, either. Blake was not the man for her, so with their wild chemistry, she was running risks every time she was with him.

Finish this job for him, go home and never look back. That's what she needed to do. She didn't want a broken heart, didn't want to fall in love with a man who would spend his life on revenge, a cynical man who was set on getting even with his father instead of trying to seek reconciliation.

Tossing and turning through the night, she tried to get Blake out of her thoughts. For the majority of the night, though, she was unsuccessful.

On Tuesday Lucinda and Eli arrived, and Sierra spent a busy day working with them as they took measurements and discussed possibilities.

That night Blake returned from his work out on the ranch and met with them in the informal sitting room, where he served glasses of wine and they talked. She was surprised when Eli and Blake found they had favorite artists in common: David Hockney and Gerhard Richter. They discussed art, architecture and furniture design. Eli left to get a portfolio to show Blake. It surprised her how attentive and engaged Blake was throughout the evening. Blake even asked about Lucinda's husband and three-year-old daughter.

During another delicious dinner of salmon, green beans, a salad and hot rolls, Blake smiled at Lucinda as he passed a crystal bowl of strawberry jam. "Next time you come—and Sierra said you and Eli will be back later in the project—we'll have barbecue. I'm taking Sierra Thursday night to eat at a place that has some of the best."

"I've been to Texas before and I love barbecue," Eli said. "I'll be counting on that."

Blake was charming with his new guests. This polite, friendly evening was so different from her first evening with him. Again, she wondered at the response they stirred in each other, something she had never experienced with anyone else.

With Lucinda and Eli present, there was more talk after dinner about various artists and buildings that Blake liked, and they all looked again at the new wing.

When they said good-night and thanked Blake, Sierra went to her room, turning in early and going over notes she had made during the day.

On Wednesday, Lucinda and Eli flew back to New York. Sierra returned to poring over catalogues.

Blake continued to charm her, talking about suggestions Eli had made that he liked. After dinner they returned to the new wing while she went over some of the suggested changes. Throughout it all they managed to remain professional.

On Thursday she couldn't keep her mind on her work. She had agreed to go to dinner with Blake tonight. Tomorrow she would fly home for a family picnic that had become a spring tradition, growing in size each year. But tonight...

Sierra stopped work at four to get ready for the evening out. The minute she had accepted Blake's invitation to eat barbecue, she'd complicated her life more. She should've turned him down, but the words wouldn't come. She *wanted* to go out with him.

In spite of all her warnings to herself, she spent more than an hour getting ready to go, finally settling on jeans, boots and a red cotton shirt. As she dressed, she felt eager to spend the evening with Blake, knowing she would have a good time and a fabulous dinner.

And later—her thoughts stopped there. She wouldn't think about his kisses, or how she should resist them. After brushing her hair vigorously, she let it fall free. She picked up a white Resistol, and with one final look in the mirror, she left to find Blake.

When she entered the library, her breath caught. Looking more handsome and sexier than ever, Blake stood across the room. He wore a brown Western shirt that complemented his good looks. His tight jeans fit slender hips and long legs, and the cowboy boots added to his height. The instant her gaze met his, she was hopelessly lost, dazzled by the prospect of a fun evening out with him.

"Wow, lady, you look great," he said, enthusiasm filling his husky voice as his gaze swept over her again. "Every guy in the county will want to meet you."

"You wanted me to meet the locals."

"Yeah, so I did," he said, still studying her and sounding as if he was thinking more about something other than his answer. "Ready? Let's go get one of the best barbecue dinners you'll ever eat."

As the sun cast longer shadows, Blake drove to Marvina, a small town that looked only half a dozen blocks long. In the center of what had to be the main street was a restaurant with a red neon sign declaring the place to be Barney Jack's Bar-B-Q.

Inside they were seated in a booth in a dark corner. There was a dance floor, but no musicians yet, and no dancers as people talked and ate, and busy wait staff scurried back and forth with trays heaped with baskets of shoestring fries, wrapped sandwiches and bottles of beer or frosty mugs of iced tea.

"If this barbecue is as good as it smells, then it will live up to all you said."

"It's the best ever."

"You lived in town, so when did you get this love of ranching and the cowboy life?"

"My maternal grandfather was a rancher. I inherited his spread. I spent a good part of my childhood there and I loved it. I loved him," Blake said. In the dim light she couldn't see any difference in his expression, but his tone of voice changed, and she suspected his grandfather had been important to him.

"So, you did have family who loved you in addition to your mom."

"Yep, my mother's parents meant a lot to me. I never met my paternal grandparents, and both died when I was in high school." As Blake talked, she watched two men step up on the stage. As they spread out to start playing a fiddle and bass, couples moved to the dance floor and in seconds dancers circled the floor in a brisk two-step.

A waiter appeared to take their order, and as soon as he left Blake slid out of the booth and held out his hand. "Let's dance," he said.

She started to protest, listening to the music and watching the few dancers. But she took his hand and stood up. In seconds they were on the dance floor, keeping time with the music. For a few minutes, it was fun to stop thinking about problems and differences and tomorrows—to just enjoy the moment dancing with a tall, sexy rancher who set her heart fluttering and would kiss her later.

For tonight, she intended to enjoy life, enjoy the Texas barbecue and enjoy Blake.

After one more dance, he said, "We should have our dinner."

"I can't wait," she answered, smiling at him, aware of her hand still enclosed in his. He took her arm as they walked back to their table where their meals waited.

The inviting smell made her mouth water in anticipation. Taking the first bite, she closed her eyes. She opened them to find him watching her. "Blake, that is the best barbecue. I didn't think any could be as good as in Kansas City, but that's right there with it. It's fantastic."

"So now you have a brand new experience—the night I introduced you to Texas barbecue."

She laughed. "Thank goodness you did."

"Hey, bro," came a deep voice as a tall, dark-haired man slid into their booth beside Blake.

They shook hands while the newcomer looked at her and smiled with a flash of straight white teeth.

"Sierra, meet my half brother Cade. Cade, this is Sierra Benson, the fabulous interior designer."

She laughed as she shook hands with Cade Callahan. "I don't know about fabulous, and that isn't my career now. I'm with a nonprofit, Brigmore Charities."

"Very good, Sierra. Maybe you can reform this guy."

She laughed with him, thinking there was a strong physical resemblance in their black hair, straight noses and prominent cheekbones. Cade's broad-brimmed black hat was pushed to the back of his head. He wore black boots and a black shirt, the top buttons undone. His wavy hair was a tangle, falling onto his wide forehead, and he had a streak of mischief in his blue eyes that made her feel he might be more fun loving and less serious than Blake.

"Have a beer with us," Blake urged.

"Will do," Cade said, smiling at Sierra. "I hear you're the best interior designer in the USA."

She laughed, and he grinned along with Blake, who

shrugged. "Yes, she is. She's modest, so I'll answer for her. Wait until you see the new wing on my house and you'll agree with me. We can make a bet on it now," Blake said. "Best interior designer out there."

"Will both of you stop," she said, smiling at them as they grinned. "I'll tell you what's best—it's this barbecue and these curly fries."

"We'll all agree on that one," Blake said. "Where's our baby brother?"

"He's around here someplace. He'll join us. Ah, here he is," Cade said, and stood to face another tall, dark-haired Callahan who also had blue eyes.

"Sierra, meet our baby brother, Gabe Callahan. Gabe, meet the famous interior designer, Sierra Benson."

"I'm glad to meet you, Gabe Callahan," she said, smiling at him as he shook her hand. She noticed that she didn't have that same volatile reaction to any other Callahan that she'd had with Blake, which was a relief.

They sat and talked, including her in their conversation until Cade stood. "It's dance time. Sierra, would you care to dance?"

She nodded, and she and Cade slid out of the booth.

On the dance floor, she turned and they began circling, doing the two-step.

She danced the next time with Gabe, and then Blake was her partner again.

He danced her around the floor and gazed into her eyes. She was caught and held, her heartbeat accelerating, desire fanning to life. She wanted to be in his arms. She wanted his kisses, even when she shouldn't. This was her last night with him for a while. She'd be going home and then to New York; he'd be leaving the ranch for Dallas. This was the last time for kisses.

It was after midnight when they climbed back into his truck. She turned slightly to watch him drive. "I had fun tonight, Blake. I haven't been out like that in a long time. And dinner was fabulous."

"I thought you'd like that barbecue. It was fun. It's unusual that both my brothers were there. I think they wanted to meet you. They didn't want to miss the opportunity to meet one of the world's best interior designers. Particularly the opportunity to dance with you after they found out you are definitely the world's best-looking interior designer."

She laughed. "That is all ridiculous, but I was glad to meet them. I'm amazed how much alike all of you look, having different mothers. It's great you're so compatible."

"We weren't always. Before Cade and I became friends we used to fight. Then we both realized how ridiculous that was, because we really didn't have any reason to dislike each other. Cade doesn't have any more control over how our father treats him than I do. He's just fortunate to be in better favor than I ever was."

"I'm amazed they're understanding about your competition with your father in the hotel business. I looked up some information on the web about your hotels and about his. You have more of them, plus they're bigger, fancier and definitely more luxurious."

"I intend to run him out of the hotel business," Blake said in a quiet voice that carried a cold tone. "I told you, Cade, Gabe and Nathan understand, and they don't object. It won't really hurt our father, but it'll annoy the hell out of him because he's competitive. He doesn't like me and never has."

"You said he abandoned you when you were a baby. How could he not like you when you were so young? That doesn't make sense."

"It was my mother he didn't like, and I was part of her," Blake answered flatly.

She stared at him in the darkened pickup and thought again about how different their lives were. She couldn't understand his drive to get even for something during his childhood, something that seemed behind him now. All his efforts were such a waste of energy and talent. She couldn't keep from thinking about all the people he could help if he put that energy and those resources to good use. With the money he used for hotels to compete with his father's, he could instead build shelters, start reading programs and hire tutors—so many easy, constructive ways to help less fortunate people.

Blake couldn't understand her way of life, and she couldn't understand his.

He parked at the rear of his house and stepped out of the pickup to come around and open her door. His hands closed on her waist, and he swung her out of the truck. For an instant he held her up easily as she looked down into his eyes, and the moment changed. Desire ignited, hot and intense, as Blake lowered her, pulling her close and wrapping his arms around her.

They walked into the wide entryway together, moving into a sitting room. Light spilled into the darkened room from the hallway, and through the floor-to-ceiling glass they could see the lighted swimming pool. But all she was aware of was Blake, who drew her closer.

Her heart thudded. Her hands were light on his shoulders as she gazed up at him. She was held by a look that made her pulse race. Locked into another electric moment with him, she wanted his kiss.

"This is crazy, Blake."

"It's been a fun night, and it doesn't have to end yet. There's more I want, and so do you," he said softly, his arm circling her waist and pulling her close against him. She slipped her arms around his neck even as she knew she should be pulling away.

All evening Blake had been sexy, fun and appealing. Desire had tugged on her senses for days. Each night their kisses made it impossible to avoid thinking about sleeping with him.

His appeal was physical. They didn't have an emotional connection. With his drive for revenge, he was a man so much the opposite of all she believed in, she couldn't imagine an emotional connection forming between them.

She could have this one night and not lose her heart.

Five

Sierra stopped reasoning with herself as she gazed up at him. Desire was blatant in his dark brown eyes, making her pulse jump. Standing in his arms, she trembled with longing. His arm tightened around her and he leaned closer, his lips brushed lightly, and then his mouth settled, his tongue going deep.

With the first brush of his mouth, her heart thudded. Slipping her arm around his neck, she closed her eyes as she returned his kiss. Passion blazed, making her lean closer. She relished his hard body and his solid muscles against her softness. Why was she so responsive to him and him alone? How could he make her melt with only a glance? Or a brush of his fingers on hers?

Wanting him, too aware they'd be parting soon, she tightened her arms around his neck, letting go of restraints and reason. She pressed against him, wanting to seize the moment. They had an electrifying chemistry that made every glance, every moment together breathtaking and exciting.

He was aroused, ready to make love. With one arm he held her close while his hand roamed down her back, over her bottom and along her thigh. She gasped with pleasure as she ran her hands along his back, tugging his shirt out of his jeans to slip her hands over his bare skin.

She shifted to give him access to the buttons on her shirt, and he twisted them free while he kissed her. She returned his kiss equally passionately.

Showering feathery kisses on her throat, he pushed open her blouse to unfasten her bra. He cupped her breasts, which filled his large hands as he rubbed each nipple. She moaned softly with pleasure. Need for more of him built with each touch. Her hands played over him, unfastening his belt, freeing him.

She ran her fingers over his warm belly, touching his manhood. Her first caress, so faint, made him gasp and shake with loss of control.

As his fingers tugged at her jeans, she leaned back to look at him. His dark gaze consumed her with a need so intense that she shivered. His touch was light and tantalizing, making her want him desperately. Swamped by desire, she wanted his kisses on her, his hands on her, his hard body against her, his heat inside her.

"Blake," she whispered, running her fingers through his hair. "Kiss me," she whispered again, touching her lips to his jaw, feeling the stubble of his beard. She continued, trailing kisses down his chest as her hands moved lower, grasping him to stroke and tease.

"Blake, I'm not protected."

"I'll take care of you," he answered, kissing away her words while he stroked her, his hand caressing her breasts.

He picked her up and carried her to his bedroom, standing her on her feet by the bed and yanking away the covers. As she caressed him, running her hands over his sculpted chest, he opened a drawer to withdraw a condom and put it on before picking her up and placing her on the bed, moving between her legs.

He was hard, breathtakingly handsome with a fit masculine body that was muscled and strong. She arched her hips, wrapping her long legs around him. He came down, his mouth covering hers.

She felt him shift beside her, and then he trailed more kisses down her throat, across each breast, taking his time, his tongue circling first one nipple and then the other before he moved lower. His hand caressed her thighs and moved between her legs.

Kissing her again, he stroked her, driving her to want him more than she had thought possible. Every touch was magic, fiery and building their desire to a feverish pitch. He shifted, his tongue following his fingers, and she cried out in need and pleasure.

"I want you," she whispered, not caring whether he heard or not, just having to say it. "I want you more than anything," she added, barely aware of what she said as his hands rubbed and stroked her, building her need.

She sat up, pushing him down. "You're driving me

wild." She trailed kisses across his belly until she took him in her mouth.

His fingers wound in her hair while his other hand caressed her breast with the lightest of touches. He groaned, sat up and rolled her over as he moved above her. She watched him lower himself to finally enter her slowly, withdrawing as her hips arched beneath him and he thrust into her, filling her, hot and hard.

Sensations rocked her, need consuming her as she moved with him.

He withdrew again, moving slowly, filling her. Her legs locked around his narrow waist while she drowned in sensation.

They moved together wildly, pumping fast in heart-pounding need. She pressed against him, crying out as she reached the pinnacle of her release.

He thrust hard and fast, climaxing with another gasp of pleasure, finally slowing while holding her close.

She clung to him, hot, damp with perspiration and happiness as they slowed. Gasping for breath, their hearts pounding together, she held him tightly. For a few moments she was in a special world, locked in his embrace.

She wanted to hold him tightly and keep the world shut away for the night.

When they were still, she ran her fingers slowly through the crisp, short hair on the back of his neck while he brushed kisses on her throat.

"I don't think I will ever forget this night," she whispered, being blunt and truthful. When he continued with his light kisses, she decided he hadn't heard her.

She knew that she would never forget their love-making, and yet she also knew she had made another mistake with him. She should not have opened herself to this man whose view of the world was so different from hers.

One night of love should not cost her heart. No matter what bond they'd forged with intimacy, she had to forget this night and she should forget him. She hoped she could do that quickly—as soon as this job ended.

She shoved aside her worries and relished holding him while he caressed her in return.

She held fast to the moment. This night was special, and their differences in priorities and philosophies didn't matter right now.

In the light of day, reason would set in and they would go on with their jobs and their lives, and she would eventually get past this night.

When he shifted, she gazed into his dark eyes, which were filled with curiosity.

"Are you sure you have to go home tomorrow?"

"Yes. This picnic is a big deal—it used to be mostly family, but it's grown. Now we invite a lot of people I've worked with, plus people—and children—from one of the shelters."

"Children? As in abandoned?"

"As in orphaned, mostly. Some were runaways and have no home to go back to, and some are from broken homes whose families can't keep them at this time, but they hope to get them back in the future. We sponsor a children's shelter."

She combed a few locks of his hair away from his

face. "Come home with me. See how we live—maybe you'll understand what I do if you'll come meet people."

"I'll be in the way," he said.

"Nonsense. There's no such thing as a stranger."

"Little Miss Do-Good."

"Scared to accept, Blake?"

He gave her a crooked smile. "Why the hell would I be scared to go to a picnic?"

"You might be afraid it will change your lifestyle," she said, teasing him, but also wondering why he wouldn't accept her invitation. "You have time to go. Come home with me. Sunday you can fly back here. C'mon. It won't hurt you to meet my family, the people I work with and the kids. It will broaden your outlook a bit."

She waited while he toyed with long locks of her hair. "Okay," he said, and satisfaction flowed through her. She smiled at him. "You can fly back to Dallas with me and leave from Dallas Monday morning to go to New York. You can fly in my private jet. I have to be in Chicago, so I'll go that far with you. You do that, and I'll go home with you this weekend," he said, studying her. "I want one more night with you in my arms," he whispered, his breath warm on her throat.

As with all his invitations, she was torn between what she should do and what she wanted to do. What was the appeal that Blake held? She had never been attracted to another man the way she was to him—it was purely physical, sexual, lustful—and she couldn't understand it.

"You're arguing with yourself. C'mon, Sierra. This

is a brief moment in your earnest, do-good life. Live a little, darlin', and stay. You'll get me for the weekend, and you can show me some of what you do. I'll see how you live, and you'll be back here to see a little more about how I live. One more day together won't be earth shattering."

She had to smile at him. "You're wicked, Blake. The proverbial bad boy all grown up into a wicked man."

"Then save me. You stay, and I'll go home with you for the weekend, and maybe the visit will transform me into an everlasting do-gooder," he said.

"It would serve you right if that is exactly what happens," she said, staring intently at him. "All right. I'll fly back to Dallas Sunday night, and Monday morning, I leave Dallas for New York. That means canceling my commercial flight."

"You'll get a refund," he said.

"There won't be any privacy at my house," she warned him. "Not only that, everyone will be busy getting ready for the picnic."

"We might find a moment alone. Tell me you don't want more kisses," he said, shifting to look at her mouth and causing her heart to lurch. The joking and lightness of the moment vanished.

His arm tightened around her, pulling her against him while his mouth came down on hers. He kissed her, his tongue stroking hers while his free hand played along her hip and then between her thighs.

Moaning softly, Sierra kissed him in return. She wanted to tell him that he wasn't fair. He had to get his way about everything, but words were lost, and in minutes her thought processes scrambled. All she wanted was Blake—his hands, his mouth and his body. She wanted his kisses, caresses and his lovemaking. She wanted him inside her, thick, hot and hard. With a gasp, she shoved him down on the bed and shifted over him, straddling him, shaking her head to get her hair away from her face.

His warm hands cupped her breasts, and his thumbs drew lazy circles over each taut bud.

"Ah, darlin', you set me on fire," he said.

Barely hearing him, she showered kisses on his throat, feeling his hands moving over her bottom and down the backs of her thighs. Tingles radiated from his touch and desire flashed into a raging need. She wanted him—his arms, his hard body, his energy.

"Where you're concerned, I don't have a backbone," she whispered, wondering how she could possibly be so attracted to someone so wrong for her.

"I thought you had a backbone," he whispered. "Let me see." His fingers slid down her spine, and then his hand spread lightly as he rubbed her bottom and she gasped, thrusting her hips against him.

He rolled her over, moving on top while he kissed her, and she was lost to his lovemaking for the rest of the night.

Friday afternoon Blake gazed out the window of his private jet at the broad channel of the Red River as they flew north toward Kansas. A silver ribbon of water followed the curving banks.

Blake figured the weekend would be spent meeting

people and watching Sierra chat with those she had helped. Tagging along was fine with him if it meant she would return to Texas with him. She'd promised only Sunday night, but that was better than telling her goodbye in Kansas City and each of them going different places.

At the thought of another night in bed with her, his pulse jumped. For a night with Sierra, he could easily sit through a family picnic.

He still couldn't understand the hot attraction that burned between them, but he wasn't questioning it any longer. He wanted her in his bed, and he thought about her constantly when he wasn't with her. Of all the women he had ever known, he would have guessed that she would have been one of the least likely to generate this fiery, irresistible appeal.

Not only were they complete opposites, he couldn't understand her outlook on life or her lifestyle any more than she could understand his. She actively disliked his way of thinking, and he thought she was throwing away her talent and her future by taking a low-paying, thankless job that would be endless work with few rewards.

Next to him, she gazed out the window. She took his breath sometimes. When he had danced with her, just a two-step, she'd had a sway to her hips that was tantalizing. He wanted to kiss her slender throat. She responded to any touch, even the most casual kiss.

He was ready for Sunday night in Dallas.

To get his mind off the temptation of Sierra, he tried to think about her family and get their names straight. He couldn't imagine growing up the way she had—a house filled with kids who brought other kids home with them. And providing for a family on a minister's salary had to have been a struggle, but Sierra never sounded as if it had been and she didn't particularly care about money. She was truly indifferent to Blake's wealth, which was something he couldn't say for any other woman he had met.

Yes, Sierra was different. She had him willing to meet family and spend the weekend in separate rooms just for one more night with her.

Once during the evening, when the noise level was high, Blake gazed at the chaos around him. Three toddlers played with blocks while kids ranging in age from elementary school to middle school were occupied with electronic gadgets. Women bustled in the kitchen, getting big platters of food cooked and ready for Saturday. The delicious smell of baked beans was enticing, even after a big dinner.

He helped her dad and two brothers load games, balls, rackets, bats and equipment into two pickups. Her family amazed him. They worked together and they had a good time, getting things done without tempers flying in spite of kids needing attention and toys breaking.

Most of all, he noticed her mother and dad, who worked efficiently at their jobs. Watching them, it was obvious they cared deeply for each other and had a strong marriage. They were constantly aware of each other and worked as smoothly as two trapeze artists high above an audience. And they were amazingly polite to each other and all around them. It made him real-ize that he had never been around an older couple who were in love and happily married.

He hadn't ever seen a family like this one. Blake's half brothers had a mother who loved them, but she had divorced their dad. She was often gone, and when she was home she seldom had male guests.

Some of Blake's friends had two parents who seemed happy with each other, but they didn't have the warmth and love that radiated in subtle ways from Sierra's par-ents.

In this big family, everyone seemed to love and care about everyone else and be genuinely welcoming to their guests.

Blake began to see why money was not of the utmost importance to Sierra. She had a supportive family. They were all there for each other, and she was grounded in that assurance. His gaze shifted to her as she came out of the house, her arms loaded with equipment. He hur-ried to take it from her, his hands brushing hers.

"I can get this stuff. This is heavy. I'll come get the next load."

"That's it for now," she said. "Thanks for helping."

"You have an interesting family," he said, wishing they were alone so he could give her a hug. "They're all very likable people."

"Thank you. I think they're great, and we'll all have fun tomorrow. You'll see."

A little boy came around the corner of the house, crying loudly.

"Someone is unhappy," she said. "I'll go help." She

went to pick him up. Blake had no idea which child he was or to whom he belonged.

As he continued to help load the truck, he watched Sierra wipe away the child's tears, set him on his feet and hold his hand. Whatever she told him brought a smile to his face, and together they disappeared into the house.

By ten o'clock that night, when most of Sierra's family had said good-night and gone to their own homes, he sat alone with her in the big family room of her parents' two-story house. He smiled at her and shook his head. "I'll never get all the names. We'll go back to Texas before I have half of them figured out."

She smiled at him—an enticing smile that flashed with warmth. "You're being modest. You did pretty well tonight. You were a hit with my dad, talking about the early days of the railroads—he loves trains and has a library of train books. I'll show you tomorrow. Right now, I just want to sit and relax."

"We can't do what I want to do, but sitting and relaxing will be okay."

"I'm not asking what you want to do, and don't tell me."

"I didn't tell you, but I think you know. I just wanted to hear you say you want to do the same thing."

She narrowed her eyes. "You're shameless."

"No, I'm fun," he answered, and her smile widened as she shook her head. "You were a hit with them tonight—even the youngest. He followed you around. I'm surprised. You've said you're never around kids."

"I have the magic touch with kids and dogs and beautiful women. Come sit closer and I'll show you," he said, having fun flirting with her.

"I'm staying right where I am. The 'magic touch with kids,' huh? When are you ever around kids?"

"Tonight," he answered. She shook her head.

"You'll be around them tomorrow. That's for sure. We'll have a lot of people at the picnic."

"You had a lot of people here tonight. Too bad Cade couldn't spend an evening like this with your family. He needs to see a family like yours and know that love and harmony are possible."

"Cade? He seems happy enough."

"All his life, Cade has vowed he will never marry because our father inflicted so much grief on so many people. He wasn't a good father to his children or a good husband to his wives. He had a string of mistresses, and I know some of them were as unhappy with him as his ex-wives were. Financially, he was an enormous success, and that's what you read about him, but with close friends and family he was a dismal failure. Cade is scared of ending up like him."

"That's ridiculous because Cade is such a nice person. At least, he seemed nice when I met him."

"He is nice, and I've told you he has a warped view of marriage because of our dad. I can't convince him. Seeing your family might. I don't know how your folks cope with all the commotion."

"This was just a regular weekend night, except for cooking and packing stuff into the pickups to get ready for tomorrow."

"I'm surprised you ever left here for New York."

"I was ambitious, eager to see what I could do in interior design—it was an exciting time. I accomplished a lot until finally I reached a point where I wanted to be here and work here. Life changes."

Relaxing, he stretched out his legs. He wanted to sit close beside her, but he knew she would prefer he stayed right where he was. To his surprise, he enjoyed just sitting with her the way they were now. Twice he heard the deep chimes of a grandfather clock from the hallway, and he knew the hour was growing late, but he didn't want to leave her.

When she stood, he came to his feet. "It's late, and tomorrow will come early."

He helped her switch off lights until there was only the dim glow from the stairs. He grasped her upper arm and turned her to face him. "Come here just a minute," he said, wrapping his arm around her to draw her close and kiss her before she could protest.

The moment his mouth covered hers, she melted against him. He held her tightly, kissing her, wanting her and wishing they were alone, back on his ranch.

When she stepped out of his embrace she was as breathless as he was. Her big blue eyes were wide, filled with so much desire that he couldn't get his breath and had to struggle to control the urge to take her upstairs.

He wanted to kiss her again, but he let her go. He couldn't understand the reaction he had to her. Seeing her family, her background, should have emphasized their differences and how foreign her life was to him. With her positive view of the world, she shouldn't have been able to hold his interest more than a few hours. Instead, she not only held his interest, she set him on fire and had ruined his sleep for nights.

"It's late," she said softly, walking away. He caught up with her and walked in silence to her bedroom door, where she faced him.

"Goodnight. I'll see you shortly after sunrise." She stepped inside and closed the door without waiting for him to reply.

Blake lay awake in the dark for a long time in a room that had to have been shared by both of her brothers because it still held high school trophies and memorabilia. He couldn't sleep. He wanted Sierra in his arms. How long would it take him to forget her after she finished the job for him and went home?

If he had asked himself that question two weeks earlier, he would have thought it would take a day to move on, take someone else out and forget Sierra. He knew better than that now. In her quiet way, she had ensnared him. For the first time, he realized he had finally met a woman who might be difficult for him to say goodbye to.

Maybe if he could get his fill of sex with her, it would be easier to walk away. He'd be happy to test that theory when they returned to Dallas.

Saturday was a warm spring day. Sierra walked into the kitchen as her mom checked on biscuits in the oven and her dad scrambled eggs. Dressed in cutoffs and a blue knit shirt, her sister Ginger set the table, while her sister Lenora helped her niece, two-year-old Penny, with her oatmeal. To Sierra's surprise, Blake poured orange juice into glasses on a tray to carry to the table. As he looked up, she drew a deep breath. In tight jeans that emphasized his narrow waist and long legs, Blake made her pulse jump. His brown knit shirt revealed muscles hardened from ranch work.

"Good morning. I'm here to help," she announced. As his gaze swept over her, she was suddenly aware of her cutoffs and clinging red knit shirt. She tried to ignore the tingles his one glance caused.

"Great," her dad said, holding out a spoon. "Come stir these eggs, and I'll see about the strawberries."

From that moment on, she had little chance for more than a "good morning" to Blake, but she was acutely aware of him as he moved around the kitchen helping with breakfast.

"Where are the guys? Are they still asleep?" she asked. "Blake, why are you the only male besides Dad who is cooking?"

"Rita and Damon's car broke down, and your brothers have gone to help them," Homer Benson said, slicing washed strawberries. "One of the pickups has a flat, and Roger and Jason are changing it. Blake volunteered to go help, and they told him to stay to help me."

"Well, aren't you nice," she said, smiling at Blake. "Thank you."

"Happy to help," he said, his words friendly even though his dark eyes held unmistakable desire.

She stirred fluffy yellow eggs, and they soon had breakfast on the table as her other nieces and nephews began to appear. They sat to eat breakfast, and Blake held a chair for her, his hands brushing her lightly as he helped her before sitting next to her.

All through breakfast, she was aware of him at her side. The family included him in their conversation as they always did with any visitors. Soon her brothers, sister, brothers-in-law and more kids joined them.

Sierra was busy the rest of the day, but she searched for Blake in the crowd, hoping he was enjoying himself. At one point, he had joined in helping with games, participating with the kids. He seemed to truly care about the children and the people around him. His actions were so different from what he said in their conversations. Maybe making money wasn't his sole focus in life. But that knowledge didn't make it easier to resist his appeal. In fact, she was getting more involved with him.

She'd hoped he would get a glimmer of what his money was doing. She hoped this weekend would interest Blake in the agency, in her father's church and in the people whose lives he could change. And he could so easily contribute. She was certain he supported charities, but she was equally certain his support was simply writing checks and letting others handle the donations for him. She wanted him to get up close and personally involved with the kids and people his money helped.

They hadn't been at the picnic five minutes when Bert appeared with Nan beside him. "We're so happy you're here for this picnic," Nan said. "And you brought Blake Callahan. That's great."

"I think he'll enjoy being here."

"How's the job going, Sierra? Do you think you're halfway through yet?" Bert asked. "We miss you here."

"The job is going well, but I miss the agency. No, I'm not halfway through yet, but I'll be home for good before you know it. Bert, will you set this basket on the long table with the red plastic cover? Nan, you can come help me over here."

"Sure," Nan said, smiling broadly. "Bert worries all day, every day about you," she said as soon as they walked away. "Nothing new there. I want to say hello to Blake."

"Say hello and whatever else you want," Sierra said, smiling at her assistant, aware Blake had local women and some of the teenage girls fluttering around him. In minutes, Nan stood talking to Blake while Sierra carried another basket of food to a table.

Along with all her family, Blake helped cook burgers. By two, soccer, badminton and baseball were in progress.

Mid-afternoon found her and Blake helping with scorekeeping and coaching kids playing baseball. Between innings, Blake paused beside her. "There's a kid sitting over there who doesn't play. He's one who hasn't played anything so far, and he doesn't engage with the others. Is there a physical reason, or something else? He's sitting on the bench with the kids, but he doesn't talk to them, and they leave him alone, too."

"That's William. Maybe you can relate a little, although he's on a different financial level. His dad abandoned them at birth, and his mom was killed in a car wreck when he was five. He's eight now, and he lives in the shelter because he doesn't have relatives."

"What do you do with a kid like that?"

"Just be friends with him. I'm not a social worker, though there is one who works at the shelter. William doesn't make friends like some kids do."

She patted Blake's wrist. "See, this is where some of your donation will help. We may be able to get more resources for these kids."

"I think he needs more than what money can buy."

"I won't argue that one," she said, surprised Blake would acknowledge that truth.

"One item your money bought is the automatic batting machine the kids are enjoying today. It sends the ball straight to them, and they have a better chance of getting a hit because when little kids pitch, the ball is all over the place. You see their smiles? We have lots to thank you for."

"Sure," he said, gazing solemnly at her before shifting his attention back to the boy who sat on the bench, scuffing his toe in the dirt. "I hope the money helps get more than a batting machine," Blake said.

He walked away, and when she looked again she was surprised to see him sitting beside William. Blake had a bat in his hands and seemed to be talking to William about playing ball.

She was busy with kids and watching third base, cheering for each child who could get a hit or run in for a score. By the end of the inning, she looked around and saw Blake showing William how to hold the bat.

The next inning, William stepped up to home plate.

She asked someone to take her place and walked over to Blake.

"I see William is going to play. That was fast work."

"He hasn't said a dozen words to me, but he listened and he agreed to give this a try. I told him that people get better when they try and when they practice."

"Whatever you told him, you got through to him. That's pretty good, Blake. I'm impressed."

"I'll be back in a few minutes. I want to move closer where I can coach a little," he said.

"I thought you said Blake had never been around kids," her mother said, stopping beside Sierra.

"He hasn't until today—that's what he told me."

"Well, then I'm glad you invited him. If he just helps one child, it'll be really good. Did you tell him that some of his donation went for the batting machine and some of the sports equipment?"

"Yes, I did. If he helps William, that'll be a small miracle, but in some ways, Blake can relate to William and vice versa."

"It's a stretch, but both of them having no dad is a common bond," her mother said as they watched William swing and miss. Blake talked to him. When William swung again, the ball glanced off the bat and was a foul. On the third swing, the bat connected and the ball bounced away while she heard Blake yell for William to run. The boy on third scooped up the ball and threw it wide, and William touched first base. He turned to Blake and grinned while kids and adults clapped.

"Maybe two lives were changed a little this afternoon," her mother said. "Blake's a nice guy, and I'm glad you took the job with him. He's going to help so many people here. Dad is already making plans about what he can do with the money you've given him."

"I'm glad."

"Here comes Justin with a skinned knee. I don't see his mother, so I'll go help him." Her mother moved away to take care of one of her three-year-old grandsons.

In minutes Sierra was busy clearing tables, and she didn't talk to Blake the rest of the afternoon. She saw him with her brothers as they joined a bunch of kids of all ages in a tug-of-war over a narrow part of the winding creek.

They had a cookout for dinner, wanting to send everyone home with a hearty meal. It was eleven when quiet settled at home, and she finally stood at her bedroom door to tell Blake good-night.

"Thanks for all your help today."

"It was interesting. I'm sure you wanted me to see what you're involved in, and you wanted to stir my sympathy. Well, you succeeded."

"Some of those kids have a tough deal."

"Are you sure Bert isn't a relative of yours? He quizzed me about how long you'll have to be in Texas, that sort of thing."

"Bert worries and he hovers, but his intentions are good."

"I don't think his intentions toward me are so good," Blake remarked.

She smiled at his joke. "He worries about me. He worries about Nan. He's a good guy. You don't have to go with all of us to church tomorrow if you'd rather not."

"I'll go and see what life is like for you," he replied.

"That will please Dad. He is always happy to have someone come hear him preach," she said quietly, looking up at Blake. Beard stubble shadowed his jaw, and his black hair was tousled. Her heart drummed because she wanted to be in his arms, wanted his kisses. She had seen another side to him today, a really good side. His helping her family, caring about people and kids, particularly William, drew her to him in ways that were even stronger than their physical attraction.

This one weekend wouldn't make him a different man. He was still bent on revenge. But it had changed the way she saw him. There was so much to him that was good.

She would soon have to tell him goodbye. She suspected it would take a long time to forget him, but the sooner they parted, the sooner she would start.

On Sunday Blake joined Sierra and her family for church and another delicious meal with so many people that he marveled at how well her mother handled everything. After dinner a lot of her family played volleyball, and he joined them, laughing and helping the little kids who joined in.

It was sundown when he told everyone goodbye. Sierra drove as they headed for the airport and his private jet. Relaxed and friendly, he occasionally brushed her fingers lightly, or her nape, or moved a lock of her hair—tiny touches that shouldn't have even been noticeable, but instead steadily built a longing in her for more.

When they landed, a limo waited to take them to

his Dallas home. Following the winding drive, the car stopped in front of a palatial three-story home with lighted grounds. Inside, as soon as he switched off an alarm, closed the door and locked it, he turned to embrace her.

Surprised, Sierra looked up into midnight eyes that conveyed his intent. Her heart thudded.

Six

"This is Sunday night, and we haven't kissed since Friday," he said in a husky voice as his arm circled her waist and held her against him.

While her heartbeat raced, she gazed at him in silence. She had always wanted a marriage like her parents' because they truly loved each other and their family. That seemed the best possible situation to her. There was no hope of that if she fell in love with Blake. He didn't know what a loving relationship was. He had no role models, no examples. He didn't even seem to want that in his life. Right now his goal was revenge—a chilling ambition.

Blake was a solitary person and probably had been for so long that he didn't even realize he was different from a lot of people. She had seen a good side to him this weekend, but it would be foolish of her to expect him to give up his drive for revenge or his lifelong feelings of resentment about his father. The sooner she and Blake said farewell and parted ways, the better off she would be. She had to cut ties with him...

But it would be after tonight.

Even as she reminded herself of all these things, she was mesmerized by Blake's brown eyes, breathless because of the intent they conveyed.

Wisdom whispered to walk away while desire shouted to put her arms around him and kiss him in return.

She followed the longings of her body, of her heart. Tomorrow she would be in another state, away from Blake. She would no longer have temptation to struggle with. She'd go on with her life and let Blake Callahan become a memory.

She wrapped her arms around him, winding her fingers in the hair at the back of his head. Holding him tightly, she kissed him, wanting to excite him as he did her, to rock his world as much as he had rocked hers.

While he continued kissing her, Blake swung her up in his arms and headed for a bedroom. As he did, her heart drummed and she clung to him tightly.

Tonight, she wouldn't think about tomorrow. Tonight she wanted to make love. Would she ever be able to forget him?

Hours later, she sat with her back against him in a large tub. His arms were around her while he showered light kisses on her neck. She was warm and satisfied.

For the moment, happiness filled her. She thought about the weekend and William.

Had Blake really been interested in William, or had his attention to the boy been meant to impress her? She didn't know Blake well enough to know what he truly felt about William. No matter what the motive, he had helped the boy, and for a short time at least, thanks to Blake, William had broken out of his shell, enjoying life and the kids around him.

"This is perfect, Sierra."

"I have to agree. I'm glad you went home with me. You may have made a big difference in William's life. Sometimes kids, even adults we work with, think they're the only one something has happened to, and William may be one of those. Although he knows there are other kids at the shelter who don't have anyone."

"How does he do in school?" Blake asked. He massaged her shoulders, rubbing lightly, his hands warm and soothing.

"I have no idea, but I can find out. My guess is average, or I would have heard otherwise," she answered quietly, scared to hope that Blake would really get involved in William's life.

"Check and see. Too bad they don't have a ranch for some of those kids who are old enough. They could learn to care for a horse, to ride, to help out and do chores. It's a good life for a kid who is willing to work."

'We're doing good to have shelters in the city. We don't have the staff or facilities to have horses and land."

They were both quiet, letting the warm water lap against their skin.

He broke the companionable silence to say, "You have a nice family. And your folks have a good marriage." He combed her long hair back from her face.

"My parents have the best of marriages. They're very happy."

"My family had more money—your family had more love. Too bad things can't balance out."

"We're all there for each other. When I quit my New York job and came home, I had everyone's support." She paused. "Blake, I'll ask again—have you ever thought about talking to your dad as an adult? It might be different now. You might find out that you really don't want to pursue a course of revenge."

"Don't try to reform me," he said, brushing light kisses on her neck, his breath warm against her.

"I wouldn't think of it. I imagine you're way too stubborn for me to reform," she teased. He wound his arms around her and cupped her breasts gently, caressing her, making her close her eyes and gasp with pleasure.

"You're starting something again," she whispered.

"I hope I am," he answered.

"Please remember I have to get up early tomorrow to fly to New York."

"Yes, ma'am," he answered in a polite tone of voice that made her smile briefly, until he twisted her around. When he looked into her eyes, his teasing expression vanished. He pulled her up to kiss her hard and then reached for a condom before he moved her over him. She straddled him as he held her hips and thrust into her, filling her, making her cry out with pleasure while she moved with him until they were in a frenzy of need.

When she climaxed, ecstasy shaking her, she held him tightly and felt his wild, thrusting response as he shuddered with his own release.

She didn't know how much time passed before he spoke softly. "When you finish this job, I want to see you again."

"When that time comes, I'm guessing you'll change your mind," she whispered, her head against his shoulder. "We'll say goodbye. You'll see."

The words were easy to say when they were locked in a warm embrace after loving. At the moment, telling him goodbye didn't seem to loom in the near future, but she knew parting and not seeing him again was reality.

When he didn't answer, she assumed he agreed with her.

It was early morning when she slipped out of bed and went to the shower. She glanced back once. Blake was sprawled in bed, one muscled arm flung across a pillow and the sheet around his waist. His hair was a tangle.

For a moment, she longed to go back and kiss him awake, but she had a flight to catch. Two hours later, as he drove her to the airport, out to his waiting private jet, she wondered again how long it would be before she forgot him. She knew time would give her the answer.

When Blake opened the car door and she stepped out, he moved close and wrapped his arm around her waist.

"This isn't very private," she said, watching a breeze tangle short locks of black hair above his forehead.

"I don't care about that. I want to hold you close."

"You still don't want to be involved in all the details?"

"I still don't," he said, smiling. His gaze lowered to her lips, and her heart beat faster at the desire in his eyes.

"I may not take another job with an alpha male."

"That would suit me just fine," he said, smiling again. "I'd have you all to myself." Their smiles faded as she gazed up at him. "I'm going to miss you," he said, his voice lowering a notch as his gaze shifted to her mouth.

She forgot their surroundings. She was telling him goodbye, and it might be a long one. His arm tightened and he leaned down to give her another possessive, fiery kiss that made her want to get back in the car with him and go back to his house.

"Don't stay away too long," he finally said as he released her. He was breathing hard, looking at her intently with desire clear in his warm brown eyes.

"Hurry back, darlin'," he whispered. The endearment shook her because he didn't say it often. She reminded herself that he meant little by it.

"Goodbye, Blake," she said, a chill sweeping her.

"Not yet. No goodbyes until the end of the job," he said. "I'll be around when you come back. We can say our goodbyes later. A farewell kiss would be good. Then we'll have a hello kiss when we're together," he said. He leaned down and kissed her again.

She finally turned and boarded the plane where she sat to watch him drive away. She wondered if he had plans to be at the ranch when she returned.

* * *

For the rest of the next week Lucinda, Eli and Sierra worked together in New York, looking at furnishings and artwork, getting together at the office to go over the day's selections, plus the changes, the sketches and suggested purchases.

Sierra worked long hours looking at sketches, plans, catalogues and pictures of furnishings. During the day she spent time in art galleries, searching for the right pieces, wondering all the time if Blake would like what she did.

She missed him and thought about him constantly. She tried to convince herself it was because she was working on the design for his new wing. Late at night he usually called, and they talked for a long time about nothing important.

The more she missed him, the more she worked. Late on Wednesday night she fell asleep at her desk. Her phone woke her, and when she heard Blake's voice, she came fully awake. She was glad to talk to him. She sat back, listening to him, telling him about paintings she had selected, and sending him pictures from her phone of what she had chosen that week, even though he had said he didn't want to be consulted.

To her relief he listened, made suggestions and, even better, liked what they had picked and what they planned to do.

"Tomorrow I'll call the contractor and set up a time for all of us to meet at your ranch. We've talked on the phone and I've sent plans, so he already knows a lot about what he'll need to do."

"What I'm interested in is when you'll be here at the ranch to stay, and we can be alone."

She laughed. "You lusty, lusty man. Eli and Lucinda will be with me when I come back. Eli is excellent in dealing with contractors, and I'm turning some of that over to him. I don't know if you and I will be alone much."

"That's not what I want to hear. I'll work on that one. This is a big house. We'll put Eli and Lucinda in the guest houses. They might enjoy the privacy."

"Actually, they might enjoy the peace and quiet. However, do not make plans for me to move in with you when I'm busy, and so many people are working in your house."

"I wouldn't think of asking you to move in with me."

"Oh, yes, you would, and I'm sure you were planning exactly that," she remarked, amused and certain she was right.

"Well, I'll admit the thought crossed my mind."

Smiling, Sierra continued talking with him for another hour before finally telling him goodbye.

During the week she called Nan to ask about William. Sierra hoped Blake would really care about the kid. He had cared enough to give William some attention when they were in Kansas, but that had been easy. Now, when Blake was back in Texas, it would be a bigger task. Part of her hoped Blake would make the effort.

For the rest of the week she got a call late every night from Blake, but then he had meetings in California and the calls stopped. She knew he was busy with his commercial properties, and he was deeply involved in his work. And she also knew that she should get used to living without his conversation or company.

Sooner or later she'd have to let go because they had no future together.

Blake's schedule was packed, partially because of things he had put off doing when Sierra was at the ranch, and partly because he worked at finding ways to keep busy to try to forget her.

She was not his type, and the sooner he went on with his life, the better off he would be. All sensible thoughts, but not a solution. He missed seeing her. He wanted to go out with her again, and he wanted her back in his bed.

Blake called old friends, accepted party invitations, kept busy and resisted calling Sierra. His father had just built a new luxury hotel in Florida, and Blake had already bought nearby land and made arrangements to start construction. Blake flew out to look, staying in his father's hotel to check it out, something he did about once a year. His hotels were taking more business than ever from his father's.

But even that work made him think of Sierra. He remembered their conversations about his father. She didn't understand his motives because she had never been hurt the way he had. She had grown up insulated by the love of her family.

He had seen the latest figures on the hotels. He had cut into his dad's business so much that he expected him to sell his properties.

In years past that small success would have brought

more satisfaction than it did now. Was that Sierra's influence—or was Blake tiring of trying to get a bit of revenge for the years his father had refused to acknowledge him?

Blake thought about the kid at the picnic, William, who didn't know his father and had lost his mother. There ought to be some way to help the boy beyond sticking him in a shelter. The shelter was better than the street, of course, but there must be something that would give him a better chance in life. Blake made a note to have someone look into it.

That was definitely Sierra's influence, he thought.

How could she have had such an impact on him in such a short time?

In early April, Sierra flew to Dallas to meet with Blake and his contractor, and make arrangements to commence work. She was jittery, and not sure if it was because she was presenting their final plan for Blake's approval or because she would be seeing him again.

When she stepped out of the rental car, he was waiting on his porch. Tall and handsome, Blake looked like the Texas rancher he was with his jeans, boots and tan shirt. He came down the steps to sweep her into his embrace.

The moment his strong arms closed around her, she forgot her mission and lost all her apprehension. She clung to him tightly and kissed him.

She felt as if she'd come home.

All that she had intended to say was forgotten when he took her into his arms. After a moment, she moved out of his embrace. "Blake, you hired me to finish this job for you, and it will never get done if we don't stop kissing."

He grinned. "So? I can live with that."

Laughing, she shook her head. "Eventually, you wouldn't want to. You paid me a lot of money for this. You might as well have your new wing finished, and I've bought some expensive artwork."

"All right. I'll listen."

"I want you to look at what we've done. After I change, I'll get things set up in the office you said I can use."

It was late afternoon before she emerged from her shower, dressed in stone-washed jeans, boots and a blue knit shirt. She left her hair loose and went to find Blake.

She brought him into the office where she had sketches spread on a long table along with 3D designs on her iPad. Blake studied them quietly. "Look through the iPad for pictures of how the artwork, sculptures and furniture for each suite will look. Go ahead." She stood by the table, watching for his reaction.

"This is perfect, Sierra," he said, pointing to a sketch of a bedroom. "This will be my room." He closed the distance between them to place his hands on her shoulders. "I knew you'd do the best possible job."

Warmed by his praise, she smiled. "Thank you! I'm thrilled you're happy with it, and I'll let Lucinda and Eli know because they deserve as much credit. They are really good at this."

"This is just perfect," he said, studying her. "I don't know how the hell you can leave a career you're perfect for. Do you know how many people would like to have half the talent you do, and they're in the business? You selected what I would have selected," he said, turning to look at her intently. "That's interesting, Sierra, because we don't see eye to eye on anything else in life. Well, maybe a few things."

She ignored his flirting. "Thank Lucinda and Eli. They found a lot of those pieces. They took note of what you like when we toured your house."

"That they did. These are perfect. I'm glad I hired you."

Her gaze ran over him. She could still feel her heartbeat speed up when she looked at him or thought about kissing him.

How could she be so drawn to him or find him so exciting when they were totally different?

Memories tugged at her senses, and she gulped for air. She wanted to be back in his arms, and she suspected she would be soon.

The next day Lucinda and Eli arrived, and Sierra stayed in her own suite that night. For the rest of the week and through the one following, workers were coming and going, goods were delivered to the ranch and there was constant activity from early in the morning until about nine in the evening. Blake left for business in Dallas and they talked each day, but she didn't see him.

The next week Blake went to California. Sierra, Lucinda and Eli stayed at the ranch to be available for the contractor and make sure everything was going well.

They all worked hard to get everything finished by the deadline.

On a weekend trip home to Kansas City, Sierra's worries and priorities shifted as a new concern emerged—one she'd never dreamed she would have.

She could not ignore her body—she might be pregnant with Blake's baby.

A few hours later, Sierra stood staring at the results of the pregnancy test. Blake had taken precautions, always. But she knew that condoms were not always effective, even when used appropriately. Apparently, this was one of those times.

Her head swam, and for a moment she felt faint. She sat in a chair, putting her head down, hoping the dizziness would pass.

Looking again at the results of her test, she shook her head. "No," she whispered. She couldn't be pregnant.

What would she do? What would Blake do?

She had no answers to those questions. All her life, her family, her friends, her school, her activities, her jobs—everything had been harmonious, satisfactory, even fantastic. She had a big, loving, happy family. She'd had success. She had wonderful friends, and she was in a second great career. An unwanted, unplanned pregnancy, being tied to a man she wanted and yet couldn't have—how would she cope?

She placed her hand on her flat stomach. She was carrying Blake's baby.

Panic gripped her, and she felt light-headed again. She had planned her life in the usual manner—marriage then children. It had never occurred to her that her life would not follow that pattern.

She wanted a doctor's confirmation in addition to the pregnancy test.

With a sigh, she calmed down only slightly. Deep in her heart, she knew the test wasn't mistaken. She was going to have Blake's baby.

But he was a man who planned to remain single. A man who didn't know anything about being a dad, about families or about children. He didn't even want any.

He was also a man who definitely did not want a long-term relationship right now. And she didn't want to marry him. They wouldn't be compatible—not beyond the bedroom.

He would probably give her a generous sum of money to support his child, though.

She thought about Blake at the picnic, sitting and talking to William, then later, coaching the boy when he joined the ball game. He'd never been around children, and yet he'd taken to William immediately. He'd even asked about the boy in their phone conversations. He cared, even when he pretended he didn't, and common sense told her that Blake would never abandon his own child.

Probably, he would insist on marriage even though they were not in love. With all the bitterness Blake felt toward his father, he would never make the same mistakes with his own family. Blake would do everything in his power to be a part of his child's life full-time. He'd talk her into getting married, or living with him, no matter how unsuited they were as a couple.

They weren't in love. Yet she was certain he would push, try to bribe her, charm her, or do everything else he reasonably could to win her to his way of thinking. If she did agree to something long-term, it would be a disaster. She held marriage sacred, the vows were life-long, the outcome of abiding love. She would have none of that with Blake, whether they said "I do" or avoided a ceremony and simply shared a house.

When she broke the news to him, she should be ready for an onslaught of persuasion. She knew Blake was accustomed to getting his way and would not give up easily.

There had been fabulous sex between them, but not love. She thought about her parents and how deeply they loved each other and how it showed in a myriad of tiny ways day after day. That's the kind of love Sierra wanted.

She felt hot tears sting. She had gotten herself into a situation that didn't seem to have a happy solution. Maybe with time and a baby, she and Blake could fall in love.

Wiping her eyes, she stood and took a deep breath. Tears solved nothing. She called her doctor and made an appointment. Then she stared into space, trying to make a plan. How was she going to convince him he could be a great dad without having her in his life full-time?

She definitely did not want to give up her baby, so they would have to share custody. Blake was one-hundred percent alpha male, and he would not take no for an answer, so she needed to figure out how to deal with him.

If he did propose, would it be so bad to be married to him?

Again, she thought of her parents' harmonious marriage, deeply grounded in love and care for each other. If she married Blake without love, they would never have that special union.

Maybe she was jumping to the wrong conclusions. She shouldn't start imagining what he would do and making wild guesses.

She dreaded telling him and having to deal with a strong-willed, determined man who would be set on doing things she did not want to do. She wasn't accustomed to having to deal with someone else on major decisions that affected her life.

When would she tell him? She wanted to wait until she was finished with his new wing. She'd settle up with him and know she could walk away without doing any further work for him. But she'd never be able to keep the secret while living on his ranch, working for him, seeing him every day. She'd have to tell him sooner than that. If they had a fight, a real battle over the future, she would just have to live with still seeing him and working with him.

She felt a little better because she had a plan of action—she'd see a doctor and have the pregnancy confirmed.

The second thing was to finish his new wing.

Then she'd tell him he was going to be a father.

Next week she was staying at the ranch, and Blake would be home from California. Sierra knew with absolute certainty that when Blake learned the news, he would start planning their lives and their future. This would be one dad who would not disappear. She felt certain that, one way or another, Blake would be part of her life for the next twenty years or so. He might not propose to her, but he would not ignore his child.

She ran her fingers across her forehead. She had a doctor's appointment tomorrow. Sunday afternoon at two she would leave Kansas City for Texas.

She had told her parents, and they were as supportive as she had expected them to be. She still needed to talk to her older brothers. They were protective of their sisters in a very old-fashioned way, and she suspected they weren't going to be happy with Blake unless she handled telling them carefully. At least they were in Kansas and Blake was in Texas.

She would see Blake on Sunday—that knowledge kept her pulse beating faster. Part of her was eager to see him, while another part of her wished she could put off seeing him for years. She didn't want to see him while keeping this secret and she didn't want to have to break the news to him because it would turn his world upside down.

She debated what to wear, how to fix her hair and how much to pack. Finally, the next morning, she dressed in a red linen suit with a matching silk blouse and high-heeled pumps. She combed and clipped her hair up at the back of her head.

The commercial flight to Dallas seemed short. Blake was home and knew she was coming, so there was a plane waiting to fly her to the ranch.

All too soon, they landed at the ranch airstrip. As it

taxied to a stop, her pulse beat faster, eagerness now intermingling with dread. She didn't want to tell Blake. In the next few hours his entire future would change, and she didn't think he would be happy about the prospect.

She placed her hand defensively against her stomach. She'd had some time to get accustomed to the fact that she would become a parent. At some point after the initial shock, joy had enveloped her. She was going to have a baby. Another grandchild for her parents. Her family would give her all the love and support she would need.

A baby in her life—the thought was scary, but joyous. She had taken care of her little nieces and nephews, and she loved being with them. She had a great support network and a job she loved. No matter what happened with Blake, she would make her new little family work.

When she stepped out of the plane, a warm, dry gust of wind hit her. Blake stood waiting at a car and walked toward her. At the sight of the tall rancher, her heart thudded.

A black, broad-brimmed hat sat squarely on his head, and as always, boots added to his height that was over six feet. He wore jeans and a blue plaid Western shirt. The sight of him kept her heart racing, and all she could think about was telling him that he would be a father.

She was torn between wanting to walk into his arms and kiss him, or blurting out that she was pregnant with his baby.

Before she reached the last two steps on the plane's stairs, his hands closed on her waist to lift her up and set her on her feet on the ground.

"Someone will get your things. I'll drive you back to

the house," he said, taking her arm lightly and walking back to hold the car door open.

Once inside, he turned to her. "You look gorgeous, Sierra," he said quietly.

"Thank you," she answered.

"I'm glad you're here. When the new wing is finished, I want to have a party. You can invite your family, and I'll invite mine. I want them all to see what a great job you've done."

She smiled at him. "Let's wait and see if it really is a great job."

"Cade wants to have their family home done over. He'll give you a call."

"Blake, I'm out of that business, remember?"

"He's not going to offer what I did, but I think he'll make a generous offer for your Kansas City agency, as well as your fee."

She had to laugh as she shook her head. "I may make more money for the agency by sticking with interior design than I ever did seeking donations."

Conversation went from one topic to another, and she barely paid attention because all too soon she would be home with Blake and she would have to tell him her news.

The minute they walked into his house, tempting odors of hot bread and roast beef reached her. "Etta must be cooking up a storm."

"Etta cooked and has gone. We're alone," he said, turning to slip his arm around her waist and draw her close.

She had promised herself she would show some resistance to him this time, but the minute he touched her and she looked into his brown eyes, she couldn't tell him no. She leaned into him, as he pulled her closer and kissed her.

She was lost in his kiss, swept up in desire that made her tremble. At the same time a pang hit her. If only they had love in their relationship, how wonderful the next few hours would be. The best news in the world was a baby when there was love and a union of two people who wanted to be together the rest of their lives. Instead, the news would be an earthquake hitting his life.

His arms tightened, and he held her close with one arm while his other hand caressed her. He took the clip from her hair, letting it fall over her shoulders.

"I wasn't going to do this," she whispered, not caring whether he heard her or not.

"I was—I've dreamed of this moment since the day I told you goodbye in Dallas. I want you in my arms, in my bed. I want to kiss and touch you, love you for hours. I've dreamed about you every night you've been gone," he whispered, and her heart pounded.

"Why do we have to be so different?" she asked, agonizing over what was coming and the monumental differences between them.

"Differences that dazzle me," he whispered. "You look fabulous. I've missed you," he added. Under other circumstances, his words would have thrilled her, but now she worried his feelings toward her would change with her news. She didn't know how angry or unhappy he might be. She was certain he wouldn't welcome it with joy.

His kiss drove all her worries away. She was swept up in desire, wanting to hold and kiss him, feeling as if this might be the last time. Even so, she knew she couldn't hold in the news any longer.

In minutes she leaned away to look up at him. "Blake, wait a moment. We should talk."

"There isn't anything as important as kissing you," he whispered, brushing her lips with his. She pushed against his shoulders lightly and stepped out of his embrace.

"There is something as important," she said. He stared at her a moment and nodded, and she knew she had his attention.

She had put off telling him as long as she could. Standing by the window as the sun slipped below the horizon, she faced him. He sat in a leather chair, his booted feet on an ottoman as he looked at her. "Something's worrying you. What is it? Can I help?"

"You can help," she said quietly. "Listen to me, be patient and let's try to cooperate."

She saw the flicker in his eyes and knew he realized he was somehow involved in whatever worried her.

"I don't know how to tell you except to just say it— Blake, I'm pregnant, and it's your baby."

Seven

Blake felt as if he'd had the breath knocked from him. Dazed, he stared at her. "I'm going to be a dad," he said. He hadn't meant to say it out loud.

"Yes, you are. We have a long time to sort things out and decide what we'll do, so all you need to do right now is get used to the idea. It's a big, unexpected shock," she said, sitting quietly and letting him think.

"I used a condom every time," he said, more to himself than to her. He had gotten Sierra pregnant. They would be tied together for the next eighteen years. They would never view life the same way, but he was certain she wouldn't want to marry him any more than he wanted to marry her.

But how else would he be the kind of father his own never was?

He raked his fingers through his hair and stood, going to the kitchen and getting a beer, more to move around than to have something to drink. He walked to a window to gaze outside. The daylight was growing dim and night was creeping in, changing the landscape.

He knew he would never forget this moment. He was going to be a father. The idea shook him. He had dimly thought that someday he would marry, someday he would have a family, but it was in the distant future, a fuzzy prospect that had held no reality for him until now.

He was going to have a baby. When he glanced at her, Sierra sat looking at her fingernails, remaining quiet while he absorbed the news.

He was thankful for that. Thankful she wasn't in tears or yelling at him or asking him what they would do. He focused more on her and wondered what she thought. She had already known about this. She looked calm, poised, and she had obviously adjusted to the idea. He thought of her big family and knew she would have their support. Blake realized if he walked away now, her family would be there for her.

Not that he intended to walk away or abandon her. He thought about his father. He would never be a father like the one he'd had. He wouldn't abandon or reject his own child, not ever. There was one way to put himself in his child's life forever—marry Sierra. That seemed to be the only solution to being a real dad to his child.

Blake's gaze shifted back to Sierra who looked up, giving him a level stare.

He crossed the room to face her. "You caught me by surprise."

"I knew I would. There was no way to avoid that."

"You're very calm about this," he said, looking into wide blue eyes, and he realized she had passed the point of shock and was thinking calmly about the situation.

"It won't help to get hysterical," she said.

"Damn straight on that. I'm thankful you're not."

"We'll have to make decisions and work things out, but we don't have to do anything right now except adjust to the idea. I think we should take a little time before we start trying to figure out what we'll do."

"It all looks simple to me."

"Blake," she interrupted, shaking her head. "Don't propose."

"I don't see why not," he said, startled that she wouldn't even discuss marriage. "You know your family will want us to marry."

"None of them will if they know I don't want to. You and I are opposites. I don't like your work, and you don't like mine."

"That's nine to five, and we can get around that," he said, surprised she let their jobs be the reason for rejecting what would be best for their child. "Our jobs will have little to do with life at home," he said.

"For us and our chosen fields, it has everything to do with life at home. I may want to foster kids or find homes for more dogs. We'll work something out, I'm sure, because we're both willing, but it isn't going to be marriage."

Shocked, because she seemed so firm in her refusal,

he stared at her. "I want to be part of my child's life," he said, trying to hang on to his temper.

"You will be. I promise. I want you to be. But that doesn't mean we have to be married."

"Damn, Sierra." Once the idea had presented itself, it hadn't occurred to him that she would reject his proposal, at least not under the circumstances. She sat calmly facing him, her long legs crossed at the ankles and her hands in her lap. She looked composed and determined. He suspected he was going to find out how strong-willed she could be.

"You don't want to marry. You made that clear," she added.

"My life has changed since I said that. I was single and not expecting to become a father. I want to know my baby, to be with him or her every day I'm not away for work. There is no way I'm going to be the father that mine was and abandon my child. I can promise you that," he said, determined that he would not let her stop him from being the father his child needed. "I want to take care of both of you. The easiest way to do that is if we marry. If we try, we can make marriage work."

"This is a knee-jerk reaction, Blake. We don't have to decide today, this week or this month, so let's consider the possibilities. I know you want to be a dad to your child, and I want that. I want to be a mom to our child. We don't have to marry to be parents, or even to be good parents."

"You're not being sensible," he said, his gaze running over her.

"I'm not being sensible?" she snapped, her eyes narrowing. "I'm the one being the most sensible. We're opposites, Blake. Marriage won't work. We're not in love."

"Marriage can be a partnership. It's something we can work at. We can get along. If we share a child, we can probably get along even better than now."

"I can't believe you're saying that," she said. "You've dedicated your life to increasing your fortune because you want to get back at your father. You're concentrating on competing with him just to ruin his business. That's revenge.

"Revenge drives you, Blake. Not love. Meanwhile, I'm trying to save people. I'm not marrying someone who is driven by revenge for childhood hurts. I'm sorry for what you went through, but there's a better way."

"That may seem foolish to you because you had an abundance of love and attention, but having a father abandon you hurts, Sierra, and it's the kind of hurt you never forget. It's not a silly childhood notion."

"I know that, but you're grown now. Move on and do some good in the world," she said.

"I believe you have a very sizable check from me that will do some good. Don't forget that," he said.

She was being stubborn. They had a fabulous relationship, and if she would give it a chance, they could work out something that would give their baby both a mom and a dad.

"I only have that check because it was a bribe. You wanted me for this job, and you wanted me in your bed. You said you were attracted to me, and you wanted to see me again."

"Yeah, I did. And you acted glad to take both checks I gave you, and glad to be in my bed," he said.

Her cheeks grew red, and he suspected she was trying to hold her temper just as he was. She stood and clenched her fists. "I think we should call it a night and cool down. I have a lot to do tomorrow, and you're leaving town. We can talk later, when you've had time to think about this."

"I'll think about it constantly, and I imagine you will, too. You might give some more thought to my proposal before you turn it down. Try to think of the baby—you shouldn't turn down my proposal just because you don't want to marry me. You're not allowing our child to have both a father and a mother full-time, in a home we all share. And think of what I can provide, including my name. Marriage will make raising our child more convenient, more workable. Think about the baby you're carrying before you reject my proposal."

"I'll do that, Blake. I *have* done that. There is nothing about a loveless marriage that would be good for our child! Look at us now—you think this would be good for a child to be part of our squabbling? I don't think so." She took a deep breath. "I think we've talked enough tonight. I'm going to my suite before we say something one of us will really regret."

She brushed past him and hurried into the hall. Her back tingled because she felt his gaze on her as she left the room.

Anger and hurt filled her. Why had she ever been so wildly attracted to Blake? Worse, why had she succumbed to his kisses and then to his lovemaking?

Now there would be no way to forget him. She was tied to him for the rest of her life. Her anger grew. She had tried to be calm and reasonable with him. She had expected him to propose and to insist on her accepting. She had no intention of marrying a man who was building a hotel chain with the sole purpose of getting back at his father. In the privacy of her bedroom she paced the floor, not only angry at herself but that Blake wouldn't stop and think before he started pushing for marriage. Yes, that had been her first thought, too, but if he would give the future some thought, she expected he would come to the same conclusion she had—they were not compatible out of bed, and they shouldn't be married.

By one in the morning, she had given up on getting to sleep. She was exhausted and yet still angry when she thought about Blake's stubborn insistence on marriage before he had really had time to think things through.

It was almost dawn when she fell asleep, and then she overslept. As she showered and dressed in green slacks and a matching cotton blouse, she hoped Blake had already left the ranch.

She soon found out from Etta that Blake had left for Dallas, and she didn't know when he would return. Trying to concentrate on the tasks at hand and put him out of her thoughts, Sierra went to work. The sooner she could get his new wing finished, the sooner she could return to Kansas City.

As she sat at a desk with sketches before her, she paused, staring into space, remembering being in Blake's arms, the laughter they had shared. They had liked being together—it almost made her wish they *could* make a marriage work—but there was no way she could get past his efforts to get revenge. That was a solid wall that would always divide them.

In spite of all common sense and absolute certainty that marriage to Blake would be a disaster, she couldn't keep from thinking about him. He had a forceful personality, and the attraction between them, the electrifying appeal that made him unique, was irresistible. He could certainly turn on the charm, and they'd had a good time together.

With a sigh, she focused on the tasks for the day to try to move on.

Within the hour, she was lost in thoughts about Blake again. Common sense said she would get over missing him. That it was just a matter of time. Her heart was trying to tell her differently.

As the morning progressed, she kept busy, supervising placement of the new furniture and area rugs, the installation of the mirrors and new paintings. Blake was in California, and she talked to him briefly on the phone at night because of questions about the house. Each time she heard his voice, she felt a pang of longing that she tried to ignore. They were cool with each other, remote, as if there had never been intimacy between them, and she suspected when the calls about the house ended, she wouldn't have any contact with him for a while.

Finally, they were finished. Blake was due back on Friday, and Saturday morning she, as well as Eli, Lucinda and the contractor, were going to meet with him to go over the rooms. She was certain any party Blake had planned earlier wasn't going to happen now.

While it wasn't convenient to move her things, she didn't want to stay on the ranch with him after the work was done, so she stayed in the small hotel in town. In her hotel room, she looked intently at herself in the mirror.

At two months her stomach was still flat and her waist had not changed plus her five-ten height might be the reason she didn't see any change. So far, she felt well and had not had any morning sickness.

She had rented a car to drive to the ranch tomorrow. She didn't want to rely on Blake for anything—not transportation, food, lodging, companionship. Her anger with him was a constant feeling. She was certain he had not changed his mind in the least, and he would continue to insist they marry for all the wrong reasons.

It was simply something she would not do.

Friday afternoon in Dallas, Blake met Cade for lunch, sliding into a chair opposite his brother.

"Well, is the house finished?"

"Yes, and it looks great. I'll have a party and you can come see. I was going to have a big party soon—you and the rest of the brothers, if Nathan and family are back, Sierra and her family, friends. I'll have it, but it may be postponed for a time."

"Are you leaving town?"

"Yes, but that isn't why. The job is over, and I don't know how much I'll see of Sierra."

Cade tilted his head. "Are you two dating each other?"

"Yes and no," Blake said. "Yes, we were, but no, we're not currently. But we'll see each other some. We have some problems to work out."

"House problems?"

Blake gazed at his half brother. He felt closer to Cade than anyone else he knew. He had to share his news. "Okay, this isn't for public announcement, but maybe— oh, hell. She's pregnant with my baby."

"Kaboom," Cade said, his eyes opening wide with a startled expression on his face. "Wow. Congratulations, I think. You don't sound like a happy dad. I know you didn't plan to marry this soon, but you said you expected to get hitched sometime. Just move it up."

"That's not the problem. The lady said no. We're opposites in so many ways, and she doesn't think we can ever truly make it work or fall in love. Her parents have this perfect union of like-minded individuals, and that's what she wants. Plus, she is Miss Do-Good and wants me to be the same."

Cade sputtered and tried to bite back a smile. "Sorry. You're a nice guy, but not out to save the world."

"No, I'm not, but I'm not an ogre. It's this deal about my hotels and our dad that gets her."

"Ah, the light dawns. She doesn't know our dad. He's no saint. His people will just dump the hotels and go on to something else, and he may never even know you were behind the loss in revenue."

"Yeah, that's what I'm starting to realize."

"If she won't marry, maybe you're better off. Look

at our dad and all his marriages—all disasters. Sierra's folks are an exception. You may be fortunate she turned you down. She's not going to try to keep you from your baby, is she?"

"Oh, no. She would never do that."

"Well, then. I'd think you'd be a lot happier without a wife. Stop and think about it. With your way with the ladies and your money and success—most women would be screaming for marriage. They would be running to get a preacher before the words were out of your mouth. Be glad, my brother. Besides, she could be right, you know. If the two of you are opposites, why tie your lives more closely together? You can still be a dad, and she'll still be a mom, and each of you will find love with someone else."

"Why did I tell you about this?" Blake asked, frowning at Cade.

"To get some sound advice. Seriously, think about what she's telling you. You may be much better off without her in your life. She's sharing your child, letting you be dad, and that's good. An unhappy marriage isn't great for a kid to grow up watching. I can promise you that because I was caught in one—a little kid doesn't understand. I'd say you've got good advice, so go with it."

"Well, I'll think about what you and Sierra are telling me, but I think I came to the wrong person. You're warped."

"Yes, because of my father's lousy marriages. Need I say more? That proves my point."

"All right, I'll think about it. I don't have a choice.

She seems to have her mind made up," he said, looking at Cade and thinking about how cynical and hard he could be about some things in life. Usually he was easygoing, friendly and upbeat, but he had another side, too. Was it because of their dad? Was Sierra right that they could never make a marriage work?

Cade stared intently at him.

"What?" Blake asked. "Did you say something to me? Sorry, my mind wandered."

"Watch out when you cross the street. If you're that lost in thought about her, you'll get run over."

"I'm not going to get run over, and I'm not lost in thought about Sierra."

"You were a minute ago. You haven't fallen in love with her, have you?"

"No, I'm not in love, but that wouldn't be the end of the world."

"No, but if you've fallen in love, then you won't be able to cope very well with her rejection. Otherwise, live your life, love your child and don't look back. A lot of guys would trade with you in a flash."

"You're just Mr. Wisdom. I may go to a gypsy fortune-teller for advice next time."

Cade grinned. "I'm more interesting, and I know you better. You didn't even hear what I asked you, so maybe you're in love and you don't know it."

"Don't be ridiculous. I'd know it."

"You've got the symptoms. You're lost in a fog. You didn't eat your lunch. You're thinking constantly about her. If you're in love, then that's a whole different disease with different symptoms and a different cure."

"Sometimes I wonder why I talk to you. Under the same circumstances, wouldn't you think constantly about the woman you got pregnant?"

"Sure. Seriously, Blake, reconsider pushing that proposal. You'll get time with your child, and you will be a lot happier."

"You can't rescind a proposal," Blake remarked dryly. "I need to get back to work."

"Okay, bro. Take it easy and come see me. I'll drop by soon to see the new wing. Congratulations on the baby. That's exciting news. Nate's little girl is a doll. I'm scared to pick her up, but she's a cutie. With your baby, I'm going to be a half uncle—how's that?"

"You'll be a full uncle. Wait until I ask you to come help."

"Call someone else. That's not my field."

"No kidding," Blake remarked, shaking his head as they walked out together and parted outside. "The party may not happen until after I'm a dad," he called over his shoulder.

He left Cade and drove back to his office on the fourth floor of a building he owned, away from downtown Dallas.

He needed to give some thought to several things. One was his true feelings for Sierra. He wasn't in love. Were Sierra and Cade right—that the baby would be better off if he and Sierra didn't marry? If that was true, then he should back off and drop his proposal.

After considering it for the next hour, he still thought marriage was the best solution. They could make it work without love. Why wouldn't Sierra give it a chance? He didn't want to examine why the idea of coming home to her as his wife appealed to him.

For the rest of the day, he thought about the baby, Sierra, Cade and the future—and he continued to debate with himself about his marriage proposal. Tomorrow, they would all look at his new wing, and if everything was satisfactory, Sierra, Lucinda and Eli would be done. As far as his relationship with Sierra went, when she left it wouldn't be goodbye. Even if they didn't marry, they would see each other and their lives would be intertwined for years to come.

It was difficult to see how it would be better without marriage, yet both Sierra and Cade thought so.

Anger persisted when he thought how stubborn she was over this issue. She told him to take his time and think about it, but she didn't seem open to thinking about it herself.

This pregnancy was something neither of them had expected, and now they had to work it out some way. He just knew he would be there for his child.

The one thing he wouldn't consider was the question Cade had asked: Was Blake in love with the mother of his child?

On Saturday morning, Sierra dressed in navy slacks and a white silk blouse. Brushing her hair, she let it fall loosely over her shoulders. Eli and Lucinda had flown into Dallas earlier and picked her up on the way to the ranch. She'd be going with the others, the contractor and a photographer Eli was bringing, so she wouldn't be alone with Blake, which suited her. She was certain he hadn't changed his mind, and neither had she.

At his ranch, he opened the wide front door to welcome them all inside.

At the sight of him in jeans and a black knit shirt, she wished she didn't have the same breathless reaction she'd always had. He stepped back. "Come in," he said.

After greeting everyone, Blake stood talking to Eli and motioned to them. "We'll go look at the new wing that all of you have worked on. It's exactly what I hoped I would get—a fantastic addition to my house, and something I could never have come up with on my own. Let's look at all your work."

They entered the open living area with its ceiling that was two stories high. The remaining walls were off-white so the artwork would stand out. The painting over the mantle was an early David Hockney that Eli had managed to find. It was one of Blake's favorites.

Sierra thought the room was beautiful—sleek lines in the furniture, minimal clutter and so different from the rest of the house. Blake sounded sincerely happy and enormously pleased with the finished wing.

As she looked at him, she felt another pang. She wouldn't let herself think of possibilities, wishes that couldn't happen. She wanted love in her marriage, and she didn't think a union without love would benefit their baby, no matter what Blake said.

She missed him, and she wanted to finish this tour, tell him goodbye and start trying to get over him. She needed to get to the point where she could deal with him without it tearing her apart.

As she looked at him, he turned and his gaze locked with hers. Again, she experienced that sizzling current taking her breath. She didn't want to feel it or be held in his mesmerizing gaze. But she was, this time like all the others.

She turned her back to him and moved with the group to the next room. Why, oh, why, did he hold such a volatile attraction for her? They were worlds apart, and a baby wasn't going to pull them together. As far as she could see, marriage would just make things worse.

The last time she was home, she had talked with her mother first and then both parents, and they had agreed with her that marriage without love would be disastrous.

She would have felt better about her decision upon hearing their agreement, except she was certain they would support her in whatever she decided. If she had said she was marrying Blake even though they were not in love, she felt she would have had the same approval from them.

Her sisters were divided on the subject, and her brothers pushed her to marry Blake, but all of them would stand by whatever decision she made, and they would welcome her baby the same as they had all the other children in the family. She already had toys and baby clothes, presents from her family.

When they entered Blake's bedroom, she spent time studying the art, avoiding looking at the king-size bed because it would stir memories of being with Blake, even though it had been in his other bedroom. She wanted out of his house, to get away from the ranch and back to her own world in Kansas, doing the work she loved—and beginning to get over her time with Blake Callahan.

Finally, the tour was over. Wendell served trays of delicious-looking food, and the dining room table held more trays and platters. Since she had come with Eli and Lucinda, she would have to stay until they left, so she drifted around, trying to keep away from Blake, wanting to avoid talking to him.

But then he appeared in front of her. "You don't have anything to drink. We have orange juice, tomato juice, iced tea—all kinds of drinks. Can I get you something?"

"I'm fine, Blake."

"If you'll stay, I'll get you home later and we can talk."

She gazed into brown eyes that hid his feelings. "Thanks, but I have a plane to catch, and I don't think we have anything else to say to each other at this point in time. I still feel the same as I did when we last talked."

"We still might try to work things out."

"We have months to figure things out. I'm not staying."

She could feel the clash between them. Nothing showed in his expression, but she was certain he wasn't pleased. She turned and walked away, stepping into the kitchen to see if Etta was there. Sierra wanted to say hello and compliment her on the food.

"We'll miss you here," Etta said. "You come back." She patted Sierra's arm. "His rooms are wonderful."

"Thank you. A lot of people worked on them."

"Take care of yourself."

"Thanks, Etta," she said, surprised by the last. She couldn't imagine Blake had said anything to Wendell or Etta about the baby, but she couldn't recall Etta saying that to her before.

Finally, Lucinda asked if she was ready to leave, and fifteen minutes later she stepped to the door and turned to Blake.

"I'm sure we'll be in touch."

"Sierra, the new wing surpassed all my hopes and expectations. Eli and Lucinda are very talented. You've got a wonderful eye. Everything in the new wing is perfect. Thank you."

"You're welcome," she said, thinking how polite they were being with each other. She was aware that Lucinda and a few others standing around could hear their conversation.

"Lucinda and Eli have done a fantastic job. I'm glad you like everything. I have to say thank you, too, Blake. Your generosity will help Dad's church and the agency immeasurably. We'll keep in touch to let you know where the money goes. It will do so much to help so many."

"That's good. I'll see you soon," he said, holding out his hand. She had to take it, and the minute they touched she felt an electric current, a deeper awareness of him.

"I'll call," he said quietly, and released her. She joined Lucinda and Eli, who stood beside the rental car. Her back tingled, and she didn't want to turn around and look to see if Blake still stood at the door watching them.

She didn't expect to see Blake again for a long time.

Would he come around to her way of thinking about marriage?

She hurt. And she knew why. She had fallen in love with Blake. Maybe with time it would diminish.

She fought back tears, thankful that Lucinda and Eli were discussing their art purchases.

Once Sierra got her emotions under control, she joined in the conversation, thanking them for all their hard work and complimenting them on so many excellent choices in art and furniture.

Sierra kept her emotions bottled up until she reached home, a house she had rented near her parents. She finally sank into a chair, put her head in her hands and cried. She missed Blake.

She had to admit to herself that she had fallen in love with a man bent on revenge. She couldn't marry a man like that. Even more of a stumbling block was the fact that Blake wasn't in love with her. She never wanted to be in a loveless marriage.

She had gotten pregnant, and she couldn't change that. She would have Blake's baby and they would share their child. She'd have to figure out a way to heal her broken heart.

Eight

Blake sat staring at the phone. Sierra still didn't want to take his calls. They had talked a few times, but they always had the same argument, then she would hang up. He missed her, and it shocked him. There seemed to be a big, empty hole in his life. He couldn't stop thinking about her, wanting to see her, even just to talk to her. He wanted to be with her again.

He still thought marriage was a good idea. Even with their differences, marriage seemed the best solution. Surprisingly, it was something he wanted.

Mostly he just wanted to see her. Why wouldn't she take his calls? They had to talk again.

What would he have to do to get her back into his life? Promise to not mention marriage? He remembered

Sierra urging him to call his dad—would that get her to talk to him again?

If he hoped to ever get Sierra back in his life, he suspected he would have to change his attitude toward his father. He remembered her asking if he had ever tried to call his father and find out more about the man.

Blake hadn't ever gotten past his hurt and anger enough to do so before, but he began rethinking things. A phone call was a simple matter. He had nothing to lose. Having lunch together wouldn't be a big deal, and if his father said no, at least he would have tried. If he called—even if his father wouldn't talk to him—maybe that would soften Sierra's attitude.

He suspected his father wouldn't be one bit more eager to talk to Blake than Blake was to talk to him, but then Blake could tell Sierra he had called his father.

Cade knew how to get hold of the man, so Blake sent Cade a text asking for the number to talk to their dad. He received a prompt reply: Do I need to get an ambulance for you?

He fired back, Not yet.

Staring at the number, he sat a long time, still debating with himself. "So, what the hell?" he finally asked aloud. If his dad wouldn't take the call, so what? That wouldn't be a change from their relationship all of Blake's life. He dialed, and in seconds he heard a voice he didn't even recognize. Taking a deep breath, expecting the connection to be broken within a minute, he knew he had nothing to lose.

"This is Blake Callahan," he said, wondering if the man would even acknowledge him. "I feel that I should address you as Mr. Callahan. I don't know you well enough to call you anything else."

"This is a surprise," said a deep voice.

Through the years, Blake had seen pictures of his father, but none recently. Would he even recognize him? He used to see a family resemblance sometimes.

"I called to see if we can have lunch soon. I think it's time I met you."

The silence stretched between them. "I live in California now."

"I'm working out there, so that's fine. I can meet you wherever you want," Blake said, amazed he was asking his father to have lunch.

"Lunch would be a good idea. Are you familiar with San Francisco? I live in Carmel, but we'll have more privacy in San Francisco."

"San Francisco sounds fine," Blake answered, shocked that this was actually happening.

"Good. There's a restaurant that's popular—Patterson Place. How's that?"

"I'll make reservations for two. How about Thursday at noon?"

"Thursday is good. I'll be there."

"Excellent. I'll see you there." He was tempted to ask how they would recognize each other, but held off. He knew he would at least recognize his father.

The call ended, and Blake wondered whether the man would actually show.

* * *

On Thursday Blake arrived twenty minutes early and ordered iced tea, then settled back to wait. It wasn't as difficult as he thought it would be to recognize Dirkson Callahan. Blake was mildly shocked, because he looked more frail than Blake had expected. He was thin and wrinkled, with white hair around his face and streaking his black hair. He wore wire-frame glasses, which was another surprise—but Blake had been a small child the last time he had actually seen his father in person.

Blake stood when he saw Dirkson survey the restaurant crowd and pass over him without another glance. Blake threaded his way across the room and was halfway to the front before the older man spotted him and waved slightly, coming toward Blake. He headed back to the table.

Continuing to stand, he waited until his father reached him and offered his hand. Blake had wondered if his father would even give him the courtesy of shaking hands. "Mr. Callahan," he said, feeling a strange mixture of emotions that flashed through him like lightning.

In his memory, his father had always loomed as powerful and formidable. In reality, he was not threatening in any manner. Blake could see only a faint family resemblance, and Dirkson didn't give the appearance of wealth or success. He could easily be the wealthiest man in the restaurant, but Blake didn't think anyone who saw him would even remotely guess he had such wealth unless they knew his identity.

To Blake's surprise, he experienced a streak of guilt. Through all his efforts to damage his father's hotel business, Blake had envisioned an opponent who was strong, powerful and invincible, not the elderly gentleman facing him. Dirkson had to have someone handling the media, and he must be using photos from several years back, or touched-up photos.

"Have a seat, sir," Blake said politely, still studying his father intently.

"Blake, please don't be so formal. It's a little late for Dad, so why don't you call me Dirkson? There's no more need for you to address me as Mr. Callahan than there is for me to call you by that name."

Blake had to smile. "Fine. It does seem awkward." As they sat facing each other, Blake continued to study his father, noticing details, curious about this man who was a mystery and a stranger, even though they had the same blood in their veins and might be more alike than either one wanted.

Curiosity nagged at Blake. "Did you drive from Carmel?"

Amusement seemed to lighten Dirkson's features momentarily. "No. I don't drive. The limo will be waiting when I'm through. Rudy brought me here, and when I call him, he'll come back to pick me up."

"Cade said to tell you hello."

Dirkson merely nodded as he opened the menu and read. He closed it within seconds. "I've heard the ahi tuna is good here. So, Blake, you're all grown up now. I know your business is good. You've done well."

Surprised that his father knew anything about him,

Blake smiled. "Thank you. I have done well. My office is in Dallas, and part of the time, when I can, I stay on Granddad's ranch, which he left to me."

"So, it's your ranch now."

"Yes, it is." They paused while a white-coated waiter took their order, and then Dirkson gazed at Blake. "You've done well with your hotels, too." He looked amused, which surprised Blake.

"Yes, sir. I'll admit I had goals in mind when I started the luxury hotels. They've achieved a certain amount of success, and I'm moving on to other things. You won't see any more of my hotels near yours. I'll admit I had a lot of anger stored up."

He looked into his father's dark brown eyes and felt very little for the man who was really a stranger—not even the anger or resentment he'd held on to for so long. He knew very little about this man except what he had read in magazines and newspapers. His mother never talked about him, and even as a small child, he suspected she didn't want to because Dirkson had hurt her badly.

"The years go by and change a person. When I look back, I realize I made mistakes, but that bit of wisdom has come years too late to do any good."

His words shocked Blake, and he wondered what mistakes his father thought he had made and whether he was talking about family relationships.

"You and I have never talked," he continued. "I'm a stranger to you. You called me Mr. Callahan. Well, it's my fault, and at this point in life I have regrets, but I can't undo what I've done and there's no use in trying to win your friendship now. Or in trying to get closer to my other sons."

"It might be too late for us, but there's the next generation. You know you have a granddaughter? Nathan is married and has a baby girl."

"Yes. I have a secretary who keeps up with all of you and keeps me posted. I've seen pictures of Nathan's baby. I've never talked to her mother. But I've opened a trust fund for the baby."

"That's nice, sir," Blake said, wondering if Nathan even cared. "This grandchild might give you a second chance with your offspring. You can try talking to this little baby, and maybe she will at least know you're her grandfather. Twenty years from now she won't address you as Mr. Callahan."

"True enough, but I'm afraid I know little about children."

"You don't have to," he said, remembering Sierra's advice about entertaining kids. "When she gets bigger, get a child's book to read to her. Children are forgiving, and she'll like you if you just give her a little attention and talk to her."

"How is your mother?"

"She's fine. Doesn't know I'm here. She's in Patagonia with friends right now. She travels a lot."

"I admire you for the success you've had and for the competition you gave my hotels. When I realized what you were doing, I was curious to see if you would succeed, and you did amazingly well. That took some gumption and some good decisions."

"Thank you. Any competition from me is definitely

over," Blake said, feeling a hollow sense of victory. He didn't care to try to get to know his father now, after all these years and after such a deep hurt in childhood, but he had lost his anger.

"I'm sorry about the way I behaved with all my sons. I don't know any of you, and I doubt if any of you care about me any longer."

"I can only speak for myself, but after all the years, frankly, sir, no, I don't care."

"That's honest." They paused as the waiter brought their lunches, ahi tuna for his father and a thick, juicy hamburger for Blake.

"Your call was a big surprise, but I'm glad you did. You're an adult, and it's time we met. When all of you were babies, I thought money was so important. It turns out it's not that important at all. It seems that way when you don't have it, or when you're young and trying to acquire it. I wanted money and power and I left my family behind."

"I think in some ways you set an example for us—sort of what not to do."

"If it keeps any of you from feeling the way I do when you're my age, then that's good. You said no more hotels, so what will you do? What's your focus now?"

"Ranching, and I still deal in commercial real estate. I'm not giving up either of those endeavors. I have some good property in this state."

"Yes, you do. I told you—I keep up with my sons. I'm proud of all of you."

"I suppose I need to say thank you," Blake said, surprised at how well this lunch was going.

They ate in silence, and Blake thought of all the years of anger, when he was growing up and as an adult. Now that he was finally with his dad, he could see there was no longer any reason for anger. Pity was the strongest emotion evoked by the man across from him.

Sierra had been right that it was foolish to try to get revenge at this point in life. What else was she right about? Would it matter to her if he told her that he'd had lunch with his dad? Or would she even listen to him if he tried to call her?

They continued to eat in silence, and he wondered if that was really all he had to talk about with his father.

"One more nugget of advice from your elder. Pay attention to what's important in your life," his dad finally said. "I didn't pay attention in my own life, and I can't undo that now. There is no going back."

"Yes, sir," Blake said, thinking about the people who had come into his life in the past month. "Sir, there's a way you can help someone else, and maybe help some little boys who don't have dads. I've been seeing a woman, and she runs a nonprofit agency that helps people. They have a shelter for homeless children. I have her card," he said, thinking about William.

He withdrew his wallet to get Sierra's card and handed it to his dad. "I went to a picnic with her—homeless kids who live in a children's shelter run by her agency attended. Some of these kids don't have either parent. There are kids you could help with a donation.

"I didn't plan this ahead of time, but I thought of it now because of our conversation. I met a little boy at that picnic. William has never known his dad, and his mother was killed. William lives in the shelter, and he has clothes, but nothing else—not a bicycle, not a ball, nothing. You might help him or other kids. It won't be your own sons, but those kids will know someone cares. That would mean a lot to a child."

And Blake knew it was true. All that Sierra had said—about doing good, about helping others—somehow it had sunk in. There was good in the world, sometimes, and he suddenly understood her better than he had before.

Nodding, his father took the card and put it in his pocket. "I'm glad to have talked to you today, glad you called. With the hotels and all, I figured you were really angry."

"I was, but it doesn't matter now."

"You're smart to recognize that. It really doesn't matter. Don't ruin the things that do matter."

"Yes, sir, I'm trying not to," Blake said, thinking again about Sierra. "It was nice to have lunch with you. I have a plane waiting, and I need to go. Can I call the limo for you?"

"Thanks. I'll get it. Good luck, and call again sometime, if you're in town."

"You can't imagine what those words would have meant to me when I was a little kid," Blake said softly. His dad merely nodded. Blake turned away, walking out of the restaurant feeling as if a weight had lifted and some old hurts had been laid to rest. He wondered if he would ever see or talk to his father again.

He had to talk to Sierra. Had she moved on with her life and put all thoughts of him aside? Was she already wiping out memories of their time together? She could never put him completely out of her mind—not with a baby between them. But he wanted more than a child with her. He wanted a life.

But before he could strategize how to win back Sierra, there was currently one person waiting to hear about lunch: Cade. When Blake was seated in the jet, still on the ground and waiting for clearance to take off, he called his half brother.

"Lunch is over and so is the competition. Cade, he's an old man. He told me to call him Dirkson. He says he has a lot of regrets, and I believe him."

"You didn't tell him off for what he did?"

"I'm all grown up. It just doesn't matter anymore."

"I can't believe I'm talking to the same Blake. I haven't seen him in a while, but we've seen him all through the years and you haven't, so you probably notice bigger changes. Well, maybe you'll sleep better now. And maybe he'll sleep worse," Cade said, laughing. "Would serve him right, but he probably sleeps like an old dog in front of the fire."

"That's my cue to stop talking to you. My plane is taking off." He could hear Cade chuckling as Blake ended the call.

He stared at his phone, wanting to call Sierra. He missed her, and he hoped he hadn't permanently ruined his chances with her.

He needed a way to win her back.

He'd tried going out with friends, but even with the most charming ones, his mind wandered until he was lost in memories of being with Sierra. Today, with his father, it had been her voice whispering to him about William and the good he and his father could do for a child.

When he was alone at night, too many times he had reached for his phone to call her. He knew now he would never be able to move on, and he hadn't expected it to be this difficult to figure out what to do next. But then, nothing about her had ever been simple. She still complicated his life, even when she wasn't present and he hadn't talked to her for days.

The thought that he might not kiss her again gave him a hollow feeling. The thought that she might be out of his life, except as his baby's mother, made him hurt.

He hadn't been turned down before by a woman who really mattered to him. Getting turned down by Sierra felt as if he had lost something valuable. He wanted to tell her he had dropped the hotel business, that he was no longer bent on revenge, that he'd even reached out to his father. But he couldn't because she wouldn't even take his calls.

He stared into space and saw her blue eyes and her thick, silky brown hair. He remembered her laughter. He remembered everything about her. With a groan, he shook his head.

He was in love with her.

He thought about his conversation with his father. *Don't ruin the things that do matter.* He couldn't let her go. He couldn't lose her. He didn't want to be like his dad—a man filled with regrets.

Why hadn't he recognized the depths of his feelings sooner? Could he ever win her love after all the things he'd said and done? He couldn't even get her to take his calls!

He picked up his phone to call her—and got her voicemail.

There had to be a way to reach her. And a way to make her listen.

Sierra stared at the papers on her desk without seeing them. Instead she saw Blake's dark brown eyes, his smile and his thick, black hair. She missed him—and with each day she missed him more instead of less.

She couldn't forget him. She couldn't even shake him out of her thoughts. She didn't want to marry him, but this being away from him was terrible. She knew she was in love with him. And that romantic part of her wanted to marry him. But what if they married and he never fell in love with her? Would that kind of one-sided marriage work?

She ran her fingers through her hair and massaged her temples. His revenge plan still chilled her. Hot tears threatened, and she wiped her eyes in hurt and annoyance.

She couldn't concentrate on work, and she didn't think it was healthy to be so glum, but she couldn't see a solution to these feelings she had for Blake. If she could just stop thinking about him…but everything in her life reminded her of him.

How long was she going to cry over him and miss him? Was she making a huge mistake by not saying yes to his proposal?

* * *

Early Wednesday morning, Nan informed Sierra she had a call. Sierra didn't recognize the name, but she took the call anyway.

When the call ended, she stepped into Nan's office. "That was a man representing Dirkson Callahan. He's made an appointment to see me, and he'll be here this afternoon at one."

"Dirkson Callahan? Mercy. Do you think he's here because you're carrying his grandchild?" Nan asked.

Sierra shook her head. "No. Absolutely not. Dirkson Callahan wouldn't even talk to his own son. Why would he be interested in a grandchild? Besides, he has a little granddaughter. Blake's half brother has a little girl and Mr. Callahan has never made overtures to her."

"What would he want to see you about? If he's making a donation, he'd send it in the mail."

"I don't think that's what it is."

"This will send Bert into a frenzy trying to figure out what's going on. Speaking of Bert—when he checked on the children's shelter, he said Blake had sent a bat and three balls—a baseball, a soccer ball and a football—plus a baseball glove and new tennis shoes to William. He also sent new balls and gloves to the shelter so they'll have more equipment."

"That's good news," Sierra said, surprised and pleased.

"Bert said Mrs. Perkins at the shelter told him that Blake Callahan stopped by to see William. Are you still not taking his calls?"

"Yes," Sierra said, shocked and lost in thought. Blake

had taken the time to see William. She didn't want to think about why that made her feel warm and hopeful. "He went by there. So he's been in Kansas City?"

"Sierra, talk to him. You didn't know he was here because you won't take his calls."

"That's amazing that he's been out to see William. Did Mrs. Perkins say anything about William joining the other kids?"

"Yes, she did. He's been making friends. She said once he started talking to the other kids and playing with them, he seemed to like being with them. She said he's changed a lot. He's still shy with her and other adults, but not with kids."

"That's really good news," Sierra said, surprised and pleased. "So Blake did help. I'll tell him how great that was."

"So you'll talk to him?"

"I'll think about it. I'm happy for William. I might just send Blake a text."

Rolling her eyes, Nan left Sierra's office. Sierra turned back to her desk, thinking about William, about Blake being in Kansas City and not calling, and about someone coming this afternoon who was sent by Dirkson Callahan. The last was the most puzzling to her.

At one o'clock, Nan ushered in a man she introduced as J. Wilson Sedgewick, who represented Dirkson Callahan.

Sierra faced a short man with a fringe of black hair and rimless spectacles that were perched on his nose. After she asked him to be seated, he opened a briefcase. "Ms. Benson, I'm here on behalf of Dirkson Callahan.

He wishes to make a donation to this agency, particularly for a children's shelter you have." He handed a sealed envelope to her.

"It is in honor of his four sons, and he hopes it will help some less fortunate children."

"Thank you," she said, astonished, as she looked at the envelope in her hand. She began to open it. "Four sons?" she asked, remembering Cade and Gabe, the married son, Nathan—and Blake had to be the fourth. She opened the envelope and withdrew a folded paper. When she opened it, a check fluttered to her desk.

She read the handwriting scrawled across the page. *In honor of my sons: Blake Callahan, Cade Callahan, Nathan Callahan, Gabe Callahan.*

Dirkson Callahan.

She picked up the check and drew a deep breath when she saw the figures for a quarter of a million dollars.

"This is extremely generous, Mr. Sedgewick," she said, looking at him. "That's an enormous donation, and we'll try to honor it the best way possible. This will help a lot of little girls and little boys, kids that have no families. Please tell Mr. Callahan we'll try to find some way to thank him and honor his sons."

"He does not want publicity for this. I'm sure you can understand. Just some simple recognition to his sons—perhaps a letter from the agency."

"Of course," she answered as he closed his briefcase and stood. She followed him to the front door of the agency and then turned back. Nan stood behind her, and Bert was beside Nan.

"What was all that about?" Bert asked.

"I can't figure it out. Dirkson Callahan never acknowledged his oldest son. According to Blake, he barely was a father to the other three sons. Yet Mr. Sedgewick was Dirkson Callahan's representative, and he gave me an envelope containing a donation to the agency in honor of his four sons. It's a check for a quarter of a million dollars for the children's shelter."

"Saints above!" Bert gasped. "Sierra, what is it with you and the Callahans and all this money?"

"Are you and Blake engaged?" Nan asked.

"No, we're not speaking. At least, I haven't been taking his calls."

"Maybe you better take them now," Nan said.

"I have to agree. Think of what we can do for the children's shelter."

They stared at one another until Sierra passed him the check and headed for her office. "Bert, will you make a copy and get this check in the bank now?"

"Yes, I will," he replied.

"I guess I'll call Blake. I can't figure this one out. How did Dirkson Callahan know about us or about the shelter? He's never talked to Blake, and the other Callahan sons don't know about the shelter."

"Blake had to have told him," Nan answered.

"That's impossible. Blake is actively trying to destroy his dad's hotel business. I can't understand what just happened here."

She heard her cell phone.

"Maybe that's your answer. See if it's Blake."

"No, but I'll take this call," she said when she saw it was her mom.

They talked briefly. After telling her mother what had just happened, she tried to call Blake, but couldn't get him. She stared into space. What had caused the huge donation, and when did Dirkson Callahan start acknowledging his oldest son? Where was Blake, and what was he doing? Why did she miss him so much when she was the one who'd said goodbye?

At six, Sierra closed and locked the office, then drove through traffic to her small house. As she tried to eat a bowl of soup and drink a glass of milk, a car horn sounded.

Looking out, she saw a tall man with a cowboy hat on her porch. He stood with his back to her, but she knew it was Blake.

"Just a minute," she called. She opened the door and her heart thudded. He had on a broad-brimmed black hat, a navy shirt, jeans and boots.

She wanted to walk into his arms. Instead she asked, "What are you doing here?"

Nine

Blake took a step closer as she unfastened and opened the screen door.

"I didn't call to tell you I was coming because you won't take my calls," he said as he closed the door behind him.

Her heart pounded, and she couldn't get her breath. "Blake," she whispered, knowing that she loved him, whatever he did. She was tired of pushing her feelings away. "I missed you."

His eyes narrowed, and he dropped a package from his hand and wrapped his arms around her. He pulled her close, and she clung to him as he kissed her.

She held him tightly, as if she might lose him again.

How could she marry him if he didn't love her?

Yet how could she *not* marry him when she loved him so much?

She stopped thinking. She was in his arms, kissing him, and right now that was all that mattered. When he picked her up and raised his head a fraction, she looked up into dark eyes filled with desire. "Where's your bedroom?"

She pointed and pulled his head down for another kiss. He stood her on her feet beside the bed as he unfastened buttons on her yellow cotton blouse and removed her skirt.

Her hands shook as she undid his jeans. She ran her hands over him as if to make certain he was still there, and she didn't stop kissing him when he picked her up to place her on the bed.

Later, Sierra had no idea what time it was as she lay in his arms, their warm bodies pressed together with her tangled hair spread across his shoulder. His lips touched her temple, her cheek, her ear.

"You haven't taken any of my calls."

"I tried to call you today, and you didn't answer."

He raised his head slightly. "Why did you try to call me?"

She pulled the sheet higher beneath her arm. "Blake, your father made a huge—*huge*—donation to the children's shelter. It was done in honor of his four sons."

Blake stared at her. "I'll be damned. I called him, Sierra. I decided you're more important than old hurts,

and having your love is more important than any revenge—"

"You did?" she cried, sitting up and throwing her
arms around him to hug him.

"Hey," Blake said, hugging her and laughing. "Yes,
I did. Do you want to hear what happened?"

She looked into his eyes and pulled him closer to
give him a long, passionate kiss before she listened.
"Now tell me."

Looking amused, he settled beside her, pulling her
close by his side. She placed her head on his shoulder
as she waited.

"I called him and asked him to go to lunch. I told
him I wanted to see him. He accepted my invitation."

"You did this for me?"

"Yes, I did."

"Why?"

He gazed at her, his warm brown eyes making her
heart race. "I love you and I want to marry you. That
revenge thing seemed to be what was in the way. It's
gone now, Sierra. Will you marry me?"

Her heart thudded. She didn't know what he'd done,
or much about the meeting with his father, but he was
telling her he loved her and she knew she loved him.

"Yes. Oh, yes, I'll marry you. I love you, Blake."
Tears of joy filled her eyes and spilled down her cheeks.

"Hey, what's this?" he said, rubbing away tears with
his fingers. "Why are you crying?"

"I love you so much and didn't realize it until I
thought it was too late. I thought you were out of my
life."

"I hope not." He kissed her again. "I love you, Sierra. With all my heart. I want you more than anything else."

"I love you so much, Blake," she whispered between kisses. Finally, she lay back and looked up at him. "Now, tell me about lunch, and why he made this gigantic donation to the shelter."

"My father was really a stranger. I could have grabbed a guy off the street and wouldn't have felt any different about him. I was surprised how old and frail he looked. I remembered him as I had as a child, a strong, powerful man. I had already decided to end the competition with his hotels. It seemed pointless and was causing trouble between you and me."

"There really wasn't much of an 'us' earlier."

"There's been an 'us' since the day I met you. Don't tell me you didn't feel sparks flying when we met. I know better."

"I suppose so," she said, smiling at him. "Go back to your dad."

"He was kind of sad. I felt sorry for him. He said he made mistakes, thinking money was the most important thing. He said he didn't know how to be a father. I reminded him he has a new little granddaughter. He said he really never knew how to be a dad, and it's too late now.

"Sierra, I don't ever want to end up like my dad. I told him it wasn't too late, and I gave him your card. I told him about the children's shelter, and that he could be a dad in spirit by helping those kids and making a donation. I guess he decided to do that."

"Oh, my, yes he did. I think Bert was close to fainting. I have the note your dad wrote."

"Because of you, we've made peace."

"I'm thrilled. I'm so, so happy. Thank you. Blake, he sent us a huge check for a quarter of a million dollars for the children's shelter. We can take more kids now, and pay tutors and… I'm thrilled."

"Oh, I have something—just wait. Don't go anywhere and don't do anything while I go get what I brought you."

"A present? The only thing I can give you right now is a dog."

"That's not the only thing," he said, grinning slyly at her. She shook her head.

She watched him walk away and thought about the day she'd had—Mr. Sedgewick, the check, Blake on her doorstep, in her arms, in her bed. He loved her. The best of all possible days.

Blake returned, slipped beneath the sheet and turned to her. "I have to ask your dad for your hand in marriage."

"You know that's an old-fashioned custom that you don't have to do anymore."

"Why do I feel that I would make a better impression on your minister father if I did it?" He placed a long box in her hand. It was wrapped in pink paper and tied with a wide pink silk ribbon.

"For you, darlin'," he said.

Curious, she opened it and gasped as she looked at a beautiful gold chain necklace with a heart-shaped pendant covered in diamonds and a large diamond in the center.

"That, my love, is a gift from me to you because you are having our baby," he said solemnly.

"Blake, that is gorgeous. It's the most beautiful necklace ever. Thank you," she said.

"Turn around and let me put it on."

She laughed. "In bed—that's ridiculous, but okay." She sat quietly while he fastened it around her neck. She looked down at the brilliant diamonds. "Blake, it's beautiful. I love it. Thank you."

He kissed her and she held him tightly, kissing him in return. He shifted and took her hand in his. "This ring is also for you," he said, opening her hand. "Sierra Benson, will you marry me?"

She smiled at him in delight. "Yes, oh, yes, I will. I love you, Blake Callahan," she added.

"Hold out your hand," he said, slipping the ring on her finger. She looked down at a dazzling emerald-cut diamond surrounded by smaller diamonds.

She gasped. "Blake, that is magnificent. My word," she said, sounding breathless and holding her hand out to turn it, letting the diamonds catch the light and create small rainbows. "This is the most beautiful ring ever, in all of history."

He laughed. "It's pretty."

Suddenly her smile vanished. "Blake, what will I do about the agency? I promised my grandfather I would keep it going and work to help others."

"First of all, you're pregnant, so focus on that for now. The time will come when you can get back to your work with the agency. I've got enough money, and the agency has enough money to keep going. Bert can run things while you're away. If you want, you can have another branch in Dallas. How's that?"

"There will be a lot of back and forth because of all my family living here."

"That'll be easy. I have my own jet. We have cars. You'll be able to get back and forth when you want to, or bring your folks to see us. Okay?"

"Okay. You're worth making a few little sacrifices for," she said.

He grinned. "Thank heavens for that."

"I still think this is the most beautiful ring." She admired it until he leaned close to kiss her, and she wrapped her arms around him to hug him tightly.

Later, still in each other's arms, he said, "Let's have this wedding soon."

"I agree. If we start planning tonight, we can get married this month."

"If you say we can have the wedding soon, then let's do it. The sooner the better, as far as I'm concerned."

"It's not late now. Let's get dressed and go tell my family. They'll love it."

"Sure. Your folks, my half brothers—I'll call them."

"Blake, I heard about you and William—that you do-nated baseballs, a bat and a glove—lots of equipment for him and for the kids. That was wonderful."

"I wanted to. I'd like to have him out to the ranch sometime. I suppose it's inevitable that we'll have all those kids out. I'll charter a bus or fly them there."

"We'll figure it out. That would be wonderful."

"This means I need to hire you and Eli and Lucinda and my contractor again. Now we'll need a nursery in the new wing, and we'll need a nursery in my Dallas home, too, unless you don't like that house."

"That is a gorgeous mansion. Of course I like it. And, yes, we'll need a nursery both places, but that's doable. Now let's shower, dress and go see my family. I can't wait to tell them. They'll be so happy for us. You'll see."

Hugging her tightly, he looked down at her. "You've given me faith in people, Sierra. I have never seen a married couple so filled with care and love for each other as your parents—I really didn't think that was possible. Because of you, I know there is good in people. I guess that rose-colored view is contagious—or is it just that I'm so in love that you've made me believe, and I see good everywhere now?"

She held him tightly. "I love you. Your life is going to change in lots of ways, but it will all be good."

"What's really good is kissing you," he said in a husky voice.

And he kissed away her response.

Epilogue

Sierra stood in the foyer with her arm linked through her older brother's. The church was packed with every seat filled, and an overflow crowd watched on big screens set up in other rooms while some just waited outside.

She looked at the row of bridesmaids. The last one was going down the aisle now. They were in pale yellow silk dresses and carried bouquets of spring flowers. Her oldest sister, Ginger, was her matron of honor, and there were eight attendants. The groomsmen were two of Blake's half brothers and his friends. Cade was the best man. Two five-year-old nieces, Viola and Tina, were flower girls. Sierra's gaze slipped past them and went to her tall, handsome rancher fiancé. In a black tux, Blake took her breath away.

She wanted to be finished with their vows and the

party and to be in his arms. She thought of all the joy Blake had brought into their family and the families of others through his donation to the agency, and she thought of how he had stopped holding on to the hurt he had experienced as a child.

On the groom's side of the church, she saw Blake's father sitting straight backed, facing his son. He was a solitary figure, and he looked as frail to her as he must have looked to Blake. She was surprised he was present.

Brad Benson squeezed her arm. "You look beautiful, Sierra. Dad told me to tell you that he just hopes you have what he and Mom do. He told me that when I married, too."

She smiled at her older brother and looked at her father, standing near the altar rail in his robe, waiting to say the vows that she and Blake would repeat.

She was filled with love for her dad, thinking what a contrast he was to the father Blake had.

"Blake's a good guy," Brad said, and she smiled.

The wedding planner shook her veil lightly. "Now, it's time," she said, and Sierra walked down the aisle with her brother to have her hand placed in Blake's.

Blake smiled at her as she stepped beside him, and they moved forward to face her father, who smiled at her before beginning the ceremony.

When they were man and wife, trumpets and organ music filled the church. Then they walked back up the aisle and into the foyer.

"Now we circle around to come back for pictures," she said, leading him through the church that was as familiar to her as her home.

The reception was at the country club. Blake had reserved the entire place. A band played in the ballroom, and there were tables of food in various rooms. People filled the club—friends and people Sierra had helped, relatives and employees, cowboys from Blake's ranch.

The party commenced, and Sierra only saw Blake across the room until it was time to cut the cake. Then they were again separated to talk to guests until the first dance.

Music became lively as the dance floor opened to the crowd, and arms waved in the air while people danced and sang.

Blake took Sierra to one side. "Think we'll be missed if we step into the library?"

She laughed. "Yes, we'll be missed. Let's go back and party for the next hour, and then maybe we'll disappear."

He glanced around. "There's no one out here right now." He kissed away her answer, and she kissed him in return.

"I can't believe we've been here alone this long. C'mon and join the fun," she said, taking his hand and returning to the dance floor to join the festivities.

Later she stood in a big circle with Blake's arm around her waist. Cade was there, and Gabe. She had finally met Nathan, but he and Lydia had left early to take baby Amelia home.

She was glad for Blake that his half brothers had made him part of their family, and she was thankful that their own baby would be welcomed by her big family.

Her sister Lenora came to get her. "It's time to toss your garter to the bachelors," she told Sierra.

"All right," Gabe said, laughing. "C'mon, Cade. That's us."

"Not me," Cade said, laughing with him and shaking his head. "No marriage in my future, bro. Sierra, throw it right to him, and we'll get my wild little brother married off."

She nodded and turned, feeling her white satin skirt swirl around her ankles.

When she tossed it, Gabe jumped into the air and grabbed it, grinning and waving it while he whooped with glee. She had to laugh. He had an exuberance that seemed to run in the family.

Friends turned to talk to her, and she forgot about Gabe. When she rejoined Blake, he slipped his arm around her waist as they stood in a circle talking to friends.

"I'm not the only one to make peace with my dad—there's my mom sitting by him."

Sierra had just met Veronica Callahan, Blake's mother, the previous week because she had finally arrived in Texas for the wedding. Now Sierra looked at the slender woman, whose white hair was turned under to frame her face. She was tall and attractive, with dark brown eyes that Blake had inherited. She sat at a table with Blake's father.

Nearby, Crystal Callahan, divorced from Dirkson and mother of Cade, Nathan and Gabe, was with a group of friends at another table.

"Let me see if I have this straight. Your dad's first wife isn't here, and they had no children."

"That's right."

"Your mom was his second wife, and she's sitting with him now. And she's very nice, Blake. I really like her."

"She likes you, and she is so excited to become a grandmother." He looked to where his mother sat with his father. "I don't think they've spoken since I was a little kid. Maybe he's made peace with her, too."

Sierra smiled. "I know your mother is very excited to be a grandmother. I've already received half a dozen presents for the baby. And back to wives—your half brothers' mother is Crystal, enjoying herself with friends and divorced from Dirkson."

"That's right. After all these wives, he's alone now. He had mistresses in that lineup, too. He just had no interest in his children."

"He made that choice," she said. "Blake, we're alone and the party is in full swing, and has been for hours now. Do you still have a waiting limo?"

"Do I ever, darlin'," he said, taking her hand. "Walk slowly, as if we're moving to find some friends, and we'll slip out and be on our way."

Smiling, she did as he said, and in minutes they sat in the limo as it pulled away and left the club, heading for the airport and Blake's waiting jet.

It was night when they entered the penthouse apartment Blake kept in New York. He turned to embrace Sierra, who had changed into a pale blue dress and matching heels. Blake was still in his tux, but he paused to shed his coat and tie while she unfastened the studs on his shirt. Before she finished, he wrapped his arms around her to kiss her, and she held him tightly, returning his kiss.

Joy filled her as she began her marriage to the rancher she loved with all her heart. His hand slid over her still-flat stomach. "Our baby, Sierra. This baby will have a world of love."

"Yes, this baby and our others, Blake. I love you with all my heart," she declared, gazing up at him with a faint smile, knowing life was good and they would have a marriage filled with love.

* * * * *

MILLS & BOON®
Hardback – July 2016

ROMANCE

Di Sione's Innocent Conquest	Carol Marinelli
Capturing the Single Dad's Heart	Kate Hardy
The Billionaire's Ruthless Affair	Miranda Lee
A Virgin for Vasquez	Cathy Williams
Master of Her Innocence	Chantelle Shaw
Moretti's Marriage Command	Kate Hewitt
The Flaw in Raffaele's Revenge	Annie West
The Unwanted Conti Bride	Tara Pammi
Bought by Her Italian Boss	Dani Collins
Wedded for His Royal Duty	Susan Meier
His Cinderella Heiress	Marion Lennox
The Bridesmaid's Baby Bump	Kandy Shepherd
Bound by the Unborn Baby	Bella Bucannon
Taming Hollywood's Ultimate Playboy	Amalie Berlin
Winning Back His Doctor Bride	Tina Beckett
White Wedding for a Southern Belle	Susan Carlisle
Wedding Date with the Army Doc	Lynne Marshall
The Baby Inheritance	Maureen Child
Expecting the Rancher's Child	Sara Orwig
Doctor, Mummy...Wife?	Dianne Drake

MILLS & BOON®
Large Print – July 2016

ROMANCE

The Italian's Ruthless Seduction	Miranda Lee
Awakened by Her Desert Captor	Abby Green
A Forbidden Temptation	Anne Mather
A Vow to Secure His Legacy	Annie West
Carrying the King's Pride	Jennifer Hayward
Bound to the Tuscan Billionaire	Susan Stephens
Required to Wear the Tycoon's Ring	Maggie Cox
The Greek's Ready-Made Wife	Jennifer Faye
Crown Prince's Chosen Bride	Kandy Shepherd
Billionaire, Boss...Bridegroom?	Kate Hardy
Married for Their Miracle Baby	Soraya Lane

HISTORICAL

The Secrets of Wiscombe Chase	Christine Merrill
Rake Most Likely to Sin	Bronwyn Scott
An Earl in Want of a Wife	Laura Martin
The Highlander's Runaway Bride	Terri Brisbin
Lord Crayle's Secret World	Lara Temple

MEDICAL

A Daddy for Baby Zoe?	Fiona Lowe
A Love Against All Odds	Emily Forbes
Her Playboy's Proposal	Kate Hardy
One Night...with Her Boss	Annie O'Neil
A Mother for His Adopted Son	Lynne Marshall
A Kiss to Change Her Life	Karin Baine

MILLS & BOON®
Hardback – August 2016

ROMANCE

The Di Sione Secret Baby	Maya Blake
Carides's Forgotten Wife	Maisey Yates
The Playboy's Ruthless Pursuit	Miranda Lee
His Mistress for a Week	Melanie Milburne
Crowned for the Prince's Heir	Sharon Kendrick
In the Sheikh's Service	Susan Stephens
Marrying Her Royal Enemy	Jennifer Hayward
Claiming His Wedding Night	Louise Fuller
An Unlikely Bride for the Billionaire	Michelle Douglas
Falling for the Secret Millionaire	Kate Hardy
The Forbidden Prince	Alison Roberts
The Best Man's Guarded Heart	Katrina Cudmore
Seduced by the Sheikh Surgeon	Carol Marinelli
Challenging the Doctor Sheikh	Amalie Berlin
The Doctor She Always Dreamed Of	Wendy S. Marcus
The Nurse's Newborn Gift	Wendy S. Marcus
Tempting Nashville's Celebrity Doc	Amy Ruttan
Dr White's Baby Wish	Sue MacKay
For Baby's Sake	Janice Maynard
An Heir for the Billionaire	Kat Cantrell

MILLS & BOON®
Large Print – August 2016

ROMANCE

The Sicilian's Stolen Son	Lynne Graham
Seduced into Her Boss's Service	Cathy Williams
The Billionaire's Defiant Acquisition	Sharon Kendrick
One Night to Wedding Vows	Kim Lawrence
Engaged to Her Ravensdale Enemy	Melanie Milburne
A Diamond Deal with the Greek	Maya Blake
Inherited by Ferranti	Kate Hewitt
The Billionaire's Baby Swap	Rebecca Winters
The Wedding Planner's Big Day	Cara Colter
Holiday with the Best Man	Kate Hardy
Tempted by Her Tycoon Boss	Jennie Adams

HISTORICAL

The Widow and the Sheikh	Marguerite Kaye
Return of the Runaway	Sarah Mallory
Saved by Scandal's Heir	Janice Preston
Forbidden Nights with the Viscount	Julia Justiss
Bound by One Scandalous Night	Diane Gaston

MEDICAL

His Shock Valentine's Proposal	Amy Ruttan
Craving Her Ex-Army Doc	Amy Ruttan
The Man She Could Never Forget	Meredith Webber
The Nurse Who Stole His Heart	Alison Roberts
Her Holiday Miracle	Joanna Neil
Discovering Dr Riley	Annie Claydon

MILLS & BOON®

Why shop at millsandboon.co.uk?

Each year, thousands of romance readers find their perfect read at millsandboon.co.uk. That's because we're passionate about bringing you the very best romantic fiction. Here are some of the advantages of shopping at www.millsandboon.co.uk:

* **Get new books first**—you'll be able to buy your favourite books one month before they hit the shops

* **Get exclusive discounts**—you'll also be able to buy our specially created monthly collections, with up to 50% off the RRP

* **Find your favourite authors**—latest news, interviews and new releases for all your favourite authors and series on our website, plus ideas for what to try next

* **Join in**—once you've bought your favourite books, don't forget to register with us to rate, review and join in the discussions

Visit **www.millsandboon.co.uk**
for all this and more today!